How to
HOWL at the
Moon

by Eli Easton

xxoo
Eli Easton

Acknowledgments

Thanks to my beta readers Jay Northcote, RJ Scott, Jamie Fessenden, and Nico Sels. Your comments helped make this a better book and I'm grateful!

As always, thanks to my husband and best friend Robert. When I said 'shifter comedy?' he said 'dogs!', and he was right. Thanks, hon, for making a dog lover of me and for being my co-parent to Lola, Lucy, and Livy, three bulldogs whose personalities helped me write this book.

Cover by AngstyG.

Also by Eli Easton

From Dreamspinner Press

Superhero

Puzzle Me This

The Trouble With Tony (Sex in Seattle #1)

The Enlightenment of Daniel (Sex in Seattle #2)

The Mating of Michael (Sex in Seattle #3)

A Prairie Dog's Love Song

Heaven Can't Wait

The Lion and the Crow

From Eli Easton

Before I Wake

Blame it on the Mistletoe

Unwrapping Hank

www.elieaston.com

Readers Love Eli

For "Unwrapping Hank"

"Queen of the sexual tension, she makes us wait for the love scenes.... When the sex arrives it's always hot and deliciously satisfying and in my opinion all the more sizzling for the delay." - *Sinfully Sexy Book Reviews*

"Easton masters effective and persuasive writing, her style natural and smooth. Dialogue is realistic, the story doesn't linger inside people's heads for too long, and the narrative grabs you until you find yourself turning pages, unwilling to stop until the very last line." – *Joyfully Jay*

"I love Eli Easton's books and this one is just the right book to sit with the Christmas tree and lose yourself in. Funny, endearing, happy, loving, and it left me smiling like an idiot." – *author RJ Scott*

For "The Mating of Michael", Rainbow Award Winner for Best Contemporary Gay Romance 2014

3

"Hot, sexy, and emotional…. DAMN, Eli Easton just NAILED this one and she nailed it HARD!!" – *My Fiction Nook*

"I couldn't put this story down. The characters were richly developed, and the story was well thought out and enjoyable." – *Swept Away By Romance*

"The story just plucks at every darn heart string and leaves you with a huge smile on your face, after you've gotten done crying, of course." *The Kimichan Experience*

For "Blame it on the Mistletoe", M/M Goodreads Group award winner

"I got hooked on the story and could not keep that goofy smile off my face." – *Head Out of the Oven Blog*

"You go to work and when your boss asks how your four day holiday weekend was you open your Nook and show her this cover and tell her you read the BEST, the CUTEST, the SWEETEST, the most ADORABLE story and if you can stop giggling and get the damn "It's Cheese!" grin off your face you tell, no insist that she read this book…NOW!!!" - *The Risque Readhead Reads*

"This is a wonderful little gem of a holiday story. I enjoyed every moment I got to spend with these beautiful boys." – *Gaylist*

"The genuine fondness, admiration, and eventually love that these two feel for each other really jump off the page. I was hooked from beginning to end" – *Mrs. Condit and Friends*

Published by Pinkerton Road

Pennsylvania, USA

First edition, Feb, 2015

eli@elieaston.com

www.elieaston.com

How to Howl at the Moon

© 2015 Eli Easton

Cover Art by Angsty G, © 2015 Eli Easton

Cover content is for illustrative purposes only and any person depicted on the cover is a model.

6

~1~

Suspicious Smells

"I'M TELLIN'' you, the woman was a paragon! A saint! An angel come to Earth!" The old bulldog's cheeks quivered with emotion. The sadness in his big brown eyes was nearly irresistible. "She fed me for ten years, handed me the choicest morsels from her own plate!"

Sheriff Lance Beaufort grounded his feet more firmly on the floor beneath the diner's table, calling upon his patience. "I'm sure she was a wonderful woman."

Gus blinked bleary eyes at him. "Oh, she was! I slept at the foot of her bed every night. We were never apart, except a few times a week when her daughter would take her to church, and even then she always brought me home something special to make up for it. A box of fresh peanut butter treats, perhaps. Or a slice of cake from the church potluck."

"I know it's a terrible loss," Lance said.

He did know, intellectually. But he didn't really understand. He'd never bonded with a human himself, and certainly he'd never had to survive the death of someone he was bonded to. He signaled Daisy for more coffee, ready to move the conversation along. Normally his mother transitioned the new arrivals, but she'd had a birthing to attend this morning.

"Now, Gus, we need to talk about your situation here in Mad Creek."

"But I don't know what to do! I never had to work a day in my life. Mother always took care of me. And now there's... there's rent. And food! I should hate to starve."

"It seems overwhelming now, but we'll help you. You can stay at Mable's for the time being and take your meals here."

"Is there a job I can do? I don't move as fast as when I was a pup, but my ears and bark are still razor sharp, and I make an excellent companion, truly I do."

Despite Gus's sincere and eager words, Lance thought he looked more suited to sleeping on the couch than working a job. "We'll find you something. For now, just get used to the town and the pack. Enjoy yourself."

Gus smiled. He was a simple soul, Lance deduced, not one

to hang on to his troubles.

Inwardly, Lance sighed. Gus wasn't the first newly quickened dog to show up in town, and he wouldn't be the last. It was a common story. Gus hadn't been born with the ability to take human form. But he'd been so beloved by his owner that he'd gotten the spark. His owner, an old woman, had died. Her relatives, clueless that Gus was no longer merely a dog, had taken him to the pound. Only through great fortune had he escaped and made his way to Mad Creek. Now he was....

Looking at Gus, Lance felt the instinctual pull. Now Gus was pack. Which meant he was Lance's responsibility.

Daisy brought their breakfasts—eggs and toast for Lance and the breakfast special for Gus complete with eggs, sausage, ham, and toast. She winked at Lance as she put the platters down, a conspiratorial acknowledgment of the extras she'd heaped on Gus's plate, and his expression of pure joy when he saw all the food.

"Oh, heavens! Oh, goodness, that looks yummy," Gus enthused.

"Can I get you anything else?" Daisy asked as Gus began to attack his meal in a surprisingly delicate way. "Hon, you want some ketchup or hot sauce with that?" Gus shook his head, his mouth full.

"You, Sheriff?" Daisy smiled at Lance warmly.

"No thanks. I'm—"

His words dried up as instinct overwhelmed him. He felt the presence of a stranger two seconds before the bell over the front door jangled. He perked up—intent.

A guy stood holding open the diner's glass door. He looked around the room, ran into Lance's focused stare, and looked away again with a self-conscious wince. He let the door close, wandered over to the counter with his head down, and took a seat.

The stranger was young—probably early twenties. He was tall and gangly, had long floppy brown hair with bangs that slanted over his eyes and ends that curled up into an outright flip at his collar. His face was pale and tired, and he appeared... nervous. Add in jeans, a jean jacket, and T-shirt, all of which had seen better decades, and Lance felt a touch of unease stirring in his belly. He wasn't a fan of strangers in general. It was an instinct he had to actively fight not to be overtly unfriendly. But lately, with all of the trouble in the neighboring counties, he'd been more leery than ever.

He blinked and focused his gaze back on Gus. Gus was intent on his food, cutting off and savoring one little bite at a time, as if it would be his very last meal. Lance left his own food untouched as he strained his ears to hear the conversation at the counter.

"Coffee and…." The boy's voice was low, and he seemed to be studying the menu. "A grilled cheese from the child's menu. Is that alright?"

"It's okay with me, hon."

"Does it cost extra to put sandwich fixings on that? Tomato? Lettuce?"

"Not at all! What would you like?"

"Everything you've got. And lots of it. Thank you."

This was definitely a person concerned about money, Lance noted as Daisy went to place his order.

Lance had seated himself facing the door, as always, and he didn't want to turn his head to gawk at the guy at the counter. But he could see a side view of him reflected in the chrome front of the jukebox. His long legs were bent at the knee, and he tapped the heel of his Converses on the linoleum floor nervously. *Tap. Tap.* In the reflection, the kid turned his head toward Lance.

His heels went a little faster. Lance flexed his shoulders to make sure the guy noticed his sheriff's department jacket.

Daisy brought the guy his salad-loaded grilled cheese and a big glass of milk.

"I didn't order—"

"Do you like milk? We had a gallon about to go bad, so there's no charge if you want it."

"Oh… thank you," the boy mumbled.

"Anything else I can get you, hon?"

"Um… Do you know where's the closest place to get gardening supplies? Plant stakes. Potting soil. Stuff like that?"

Lance was out of the booth before the guy had finished speaking. He could feel the hair on the back of his neck and arms stand up with the kick of adrenaline that shot through him. But he forced himself to look relaxed as he walked to the counter and took the empty stool next to the stranger.

"Daisy, can you get Gus some more coffee?" he asked. Daisy's mouth was still hanging open as if to answer the guy, or maybe in surprise.

"Uh… sure." She took her cue and left them alone.

13

The guy peeked at Lance from under his bangs. This close up, his eyes were hazel and his face narrow, boyish, and somehow both shy and defiant at the same time. Lance found it strangely... appealing. He watched the boy's Adam's apple bob up and down as he swallowed. A faint tang of nervous sweat wafted up. Lance tried to be subtle as he leaned forward a tiny bit and sniffed.

The boy carried the scent of gasoline—he'd filled his car's tank recently. He hadn't showered in a day or two either— probably slept in his car. Below that was an interesting loamy smell, like the rich scent of earth, but not the soil from around here, someplace near the sea. And... pot. The sickly sweet smell of marijuana was fresh. Denim held on to smoke like a tight-fisted lawyer, but this wasn't an old smell.

The guy said nothing, just picked up half his sandwich, head down, and took a bite. Lance continued to stare.

"There's a Garden Center in Fresno," he said, still staring.

"Oh.... Thanks," the guy mumbled, chewing as if the sandwich might have ground glass in it and he had to be careful. His bright eyes darted everywhere but at Lance.

"Passing through?" Lance asked.

14

"N-no."

"Visiting family? Going camping? Taking a sabbatical?"

"I, um, just moved here."

Damn it. Lance nodded knowingly, his eyes still fixed on the guy's face. *Sweat visible on the lip. Shoulders hunched. Definitely nervous.*

"That so. Well, we could always use some fresh blood," Lance said, not meaning a word of it. Not that he really minded people moving into the area—as long as they weren't troublemakers. Or likely to dig into the town's secrets. "Whatcha plan on growing?"

The guy stiffened, and his head swung around to directly meet Lance's gaze for the first time. His hazel eyes darkened slightly, his pupils narrowing. His nostrils flared and the corner of his mouth wobbled.

That's fear. Lance's hackles raised a little more. He tensed, ready for a fight, or to catch this guy if he tried to bolt.

But what happened was the last thing Lance expected. The guy looked down at Lance's uniform and suddenly barked out a laugh.

"Oh, right! Cop! I get it! Oh, sorry, I thought.... But

you…. Here."

The guy leaned forward and exhaled a long and heavy breath right into Lance's face.

What the fuck?

Lance blinked rapidly in surprise.

"See? I'm not drunk or anything. Or stoned. Do I look it? I drove through the night, so I'm kinda rumpled. And probably I stink. I saw you sniffing me. But I'm not…." The guy seemed to catch up with Lance's shocked expression. He turned an amazing shade of red. "Oh. Shit. Oh, God. I just breathed right in your face, didn't I? People don't do that, do they? I mean, it's not like your nose is a breathalizer or anything. That was probably really rude. Oh, my God, I'm so sorry."

Lance was still processing. The rich scent of the guy's breath lingered in his nose—no hint of smoke of any kind but yummy with cheese and butter and bread and, below that, something human and sweet, like the smell of a young child playing in the dirt. That scent was incredibly distracting. Lance's nose wanted to sniff out more of it, wanted to lean forward and bury itself in the guy's mouth. He fought off this purely instinctual reaction of his dog while trying to logically process what the guy was *doing*.

16

Nobody could be that awkward. Was he playing with Lance? Acting dumb? Trying to derail the conversation? Pull one over on the backwater cop?

Lance narrowed his eyes. "What's your name?" His voice was harder now.

"T-um... T-Timothy. Traynor. Oh, my gosh. Look at the time." The guy stuffed the rest of the sandwich in his mouth, used one finger to pull up the sleeve of his jean jacket and look at his bare wrist. *A hair past a freckle, then.* He stood up, mouth stuffed full, made some frantic waving gestures, dug out a wad of bills from his jacket pocket, tossed a five and a one on the counter, and left.

Lance watched this little charade in utter stillness, his eyes never leaving the guy's face, and then his car—an old, beat-to-shit pickup truck—as T-Timothy pulled out and drove down Main Street overly fast, then too slow, like he'd realized Lance was watching.

Daisy came over as Lance leaned forward to sniff at the guy's abandoned airspace.

"Good Lord, Sheriff. What'd you say to that poor kid? He seemed really nice."

"Yeah. If you don't take into account that every word out of his mouth was a lie." That, and the smell of pot.

Daisy looked torn between her loyalty to Lance and her natural friendliness. She was a second genner, and had come from retrievers anyway—not a breed prone to disliking strangers. She loved everybody. Which is why she was a waitress at the diner and Lance was the sheriff.

"That guy comes in again, you give me a call, you hear?" Lance said.

Daisy nodded reluctantly. "I was gonna give him some cake on the house. I don't think he was lying about being broke. Not that he said that, but you could tell."

No, Lance didn't think he was lying about that either. But broke people sometimes did desperate things.

*   *   *

Tim pulled into the long driveway that led to Linda's house, wove through the trees, and pulled to a stop in front of the small cabin. He patted the cracked red dashboard of his truck gratefully.

18

"You are the best truck in the whole wide world, Bessy. I needed you and you came through."

He hadn't expected her to make it all the way from Santa Barbara to Mad Creek—up mountains, no less. She had 120,000 miles logged on her odometer, and that was optimistic. For all Tim knew, it had rolled over at 999,999 and kept going. She was overdue for a tune-up and oil change—a task he'd put off because of a) money and b) time. So then of course when he'd needed to leave town urgently, and with no warning, she hadn't been ready for the trip.

Neither had he. But here they were.

He'd been so worried about getting stranded in the middle of nowhere, he'd even picked up a young hitchhiker for company. The boy had been harmless but also a stoner. He'd reeked of pot and said 'dude' every third word. Big help he would have been if the truck had broken down. Tim hadn't been sad to drop him off in Fresno.

He sighed, listening to Bessy's engine tick in relief as it cooled, then got out and started hauling bags from the back. Everything he owned was in six large plastic trash bags. Plus he had one box of old gardening supplies. Those supplies were *his personally*, from when he'd owned his own gardening service.

19

You take one clipping, one seed, one plant tab, I will make sure you regret it!

He'd started that service when he was only twelve, and though he'd sold off his mower and leaf blower and some of the larger tools when he'd gone to work for Roots of Life at eighteen, he'd kept the smaller things in case he ever wanted to garden at home. In case he ever *had* a home.

He put the plastic bags and the box on the porch and looked around to take it all in, sniffed the crisp piney air.

Linda hadn't been kidding when she'd said her cabin was a bit rough. She claimed a local guy looked after the place—did some basic yard work and maintenance once a month. But it didn't look like Mr. Handyman had been there in a while. The grass needed cutting—it was probably the first real spring flush of March. There were small dead branches and twigs all over the place from a passing storm. The gravel driveway was holey and furred with clumps of weeds. The cabin....

Tim reached out his hand and ran his palm lightly over the old split logs that made up the wall next to the front door.

The cabin was home. At least for six months. The thought made Tim smile, and at the same time his heart pinged in anxiety. *Only six months.* He had six months rent-free from

Linda in exchange for inventing her a hybrid rose that no one had ever succeeded in producing, six months to set up a profitable business selling what he grew so that once that grace period was up he could pay rent. And he had to do all of that from scratch, with nothing but one old box containing a few pairs of work gloves, trowels, small weeders, and other odds and ends. He had fifteen hundred dollars in the bank. Period.

I hear of you trying to grow and sell anything, and I will sue you so fast your head will spin! You think you can be somebody on your own? You have the social aptitude of a gnat, and you couldn't run a business if Donald Trump himself was sitting on your shoulder.

Grief and anger blossomed in Tim's chest, and he blinked his eyes hard. After all he'd done for Marshall… he'd thought they were business partners. Then he'd found out that their partnership consisted of him doing all the work and Marshall keeping all the profits and filing copyrights under his own name besides. Tim took a deep breath and looked around again at the tall pine trees and the big blue peak he could see over them. The Sierra Mountains were stunning.

He was here, in Mad Creek, in this beautiful place. He had a place to stay and work for the time being. He was going to be fine. More than that, he was going to *enjoy this place*. This was the first place he'd lived in that was his very own. He was going to make the most of it.

Tim felt a frisson of fear, and his thoughts went to the diner. Everything was going to be fine as long as he didn't run into that cop again. What was *with* that? That… that gorgeous black-haired, blue-eyed man's man in a uniform who'd sat down in Tim's space, *smelled* him, and stared at him with these weird intent eyes. Tim had never seen a look like that before. It wasn't a come-on. It was more like: *Leave my town, leave now. Bwah-ha-ha.* What the fuck? For one paranoid second, Tim had thought the cop must have been sicced on him by Marshall. But that made no sense. Marshall had no idea where Tim was, did he? He couldn't. Hell, he'd just *gotten* there. No one knew he was in Mad Creek except Linda.

And then, of course, Tim had spazzed out, like he always did around people. Made an idiot of himself.

He sighed. Oh, well. He was never going to see that cop again, right?

He found the key just where Linda had said it would be hidden, dumped his bags inside, and went off to find the greenhouse.

~2~

Don't Make Me Come Over There

"OH, LANCE! You have to go by tomorrow and see her. Get her scent. She's the most adorable little black-haired baby you ever saw! Her eyes are already as blue as yours!"

Lance grunted in agreement and took another bite of beef stew. How his mother had managed the stew when she'd been at the McGurver's all day helping Jane McGurver deliver was a mystery. Then again, his mother generated food the way a wellspring generated water. It just bubbled up all around her.

"Baby Samantha is not even a day old," Lance pointed out. "There's plenty of time to get her scent."

"Oh, heavens!" His mother finally stopped fussing around the kitchen and sat down to her own bowl of stew. "I knew at first glance she was quickened. The little pads on her fingers are all plump and wide—cutest thing you ever saw!"

"Of course she's quick. Both her parents are."

"There is *nothing* on this earth more adorable than a baby quick," his mother insisted. "Like a baby and a puppy all rolled into one."

This was a common pronouncement of his mother's. She said it anytime she saw a baby quick. But they just looked like ordinary human babies to Lance. Maybe their noses were a little more button, their lips a bit more pouty over the tiny teeth they were born with. And, yes, they did have the typical quickened fingers with wide, squared fingerpads. But still. Most quick children couldn't even shift until five or six or even puberty. They looked nothing like puppies.

Lance took another bite and steeled himself for more baby talk. His mother always got like this when she played midwife.

She put down her spoon and fixed him with a look. "Lance, why won't you ask Lizzy out? She's perfect for you."

Yup. Precognition skills +1. Patience -2.

"Mother, just like the last fifty-five thousand times you've mentioned it, I have no intention of getting married and having a family. You're just going to have to content yourself with the grandchildren you already have." Lance had six nieces and nephews currently, and there were no doubt more on the way from his four siblings.

25

His mother narrowed her eyes at him. He could see her mind working on how to get him to come around. She was never going to give up, and she would be fit and healthy enough to badger him about it for years and years.

Lily Beaufort was a young fifty-five. She'd only been nineteen when she had Lance's older brothers, Lonnie and Ronnie. And she was still sprightly, wiry, and had more energy than ten humans her age. Her hair was thick and black, with a few silver clumps that grew like ribbons among the midnight. Like many quickened, she'd never taken to makeup and favored practical clothes rather than frilly ones, but she was stunning. She was beautiful without any effort at all.

She was also a royal pain in the ass. Lance had heard humans talk about the tenacity of Jewish mothers. He didn't know any, but he'd be surprised if they could hold a candle to the relentless herding instinct of a quickened mother who was descended on both sides from border collies.

He didn't meet her eyes, didn't challenge her. That would only escalate this conversation. He focused on his stew even though he'd lost his appetite.

"You're thirty-one years old, Lance. How old do you intend to be when you finally settle down?"

"Maybe I never will," Lance said firmly. "You know how I feel about it. This town is my family, it's my pack. It takes all of my attention. Plus, it's dangerous. I don't have anything left to give a wife and kids, and I won't get into something I can't do right."

"So like your father!" Lily huffed with a mix of regret and fondness. "You take everything so seriously! You'll give yourself a heart attack just like he did."

He heard pain in his mother's voice and felt a corresponding pressure in his chest. His father *had* worked himself to death, and everyone knew it. But he'd been a great man.

"At least your father had us to lighten his load. You need a bond that's just for you," Lily insisted. "The *town* is never gonna satisfy that need in you, my darling."

"I have bonds. I have a bond to you, to Lonnie and Ronnie, Sally and Sam, and their kids. I have friends."

"It's not the same thing. Take heed! Either you choose the bond, or it chooses you. I don't want to see you fall victim to some so-and-so because you've ignored your needs for too long! You need to give yourself a chance to bond with a perfectly nice quickened girl."

27

This was a new argument. Lance blinked at his mother in confusion and decided she was making no sense. He took another bite of stew.

"Anyway, it's not like we have gang wars or hordes of dog catchers invading the area," she huffed dismissively. "I don't see what's so dang important that you have to be Sheriff 24/7. And now that nice Roman Charsguard is living here. Maybe he could take some of the burden off your shoulders. He seems to know his way around trouble, if we ever had any. Which we don't!"

But Lance heard the false note in his mother's voice. Despite what she said, she was as paranoid as he was. It ran in the family. They all worried about Mad Creek. Constantly.

He thought about his encounter with that guy in the diner today and frowned.

"What is it?" Lily asked, sitting up pertly.

"'Member I told you about that shooting that took place in Mariposa last month?"

"The one related to drugs?"

He nodded. "They have a real problem with marijuana growers in Mariposa County. And now they have the drug farms fighting each other. And supposedly the Mexican cartels are trying to move in to the Sierra Nevadas too. Everyone thinks pot will be legalized in California in the next few years, and they're trying to get a foothold. We can't have that here."

His voice had grown increasingly tight, and Lily shifted restlessly. "Well... that's not going to happen, right? Mariposa is over a hundred miles away! We haven't had any trouble with marijuana in Mad Creek."

"Not, yet. But we can't afford to. We can't withstand the attention, and you know it."

Mad Creek was a sleepy little town that was on the way to nowhere. Though they were close to Yosemite National Park and Mammoth Lakes as the crow flies, they were hours away from the main attractions by car. And there were far better and more direct routes to take if you were driving over the mountains to Nevada than the little rattail that ran through Mad Creek.

And that was a good thing. Because Mad Creek had more than its share of secrets to hide from the world, and the quickened pack members, who had to be protected right along with those secrets. And that was why Lance didn't have time to fuss about his own life.

"Oh, tosh! Drugs! That'll never happen here. Besides, I pity any man who'd try to do something like that on *your*

29

territory." His mother was trying to minimize the threat, still intent on the baby campaign. But he could see that she hadn't quite convinced herself.

Lance had a sudden, visceral memory of the guy at the diner. The bright light in his hazel eyes. The long, awkwardly coltish legs in jeans, the way that one thick lank of hair flopped over his forehead, the way he'd been so withdrawn and then had perked up and gotten all animated only to exhale right into Lance's face and then get so embarrassed about it.

"What are *you* smiling at?" Lily asked with surprise.

Lance stopped smiling. "Nothing."

"Hmmm." Lily was watching him like a hawk. Or a border collie.

It was no big deal. She'd understand if she'd seen the guy. Suspicious, yes, but in retrospect also weirdly cute. Probably way cuter than baby Samantha.

Lanced frowned at the strange thought.

"Something happened that you're not telling me. What is it?" Lily demanded.

Lance couldn't help it. It wasn't often he had something to hold over his mother. As in, *never*. He braced his palms on the table and stretched, acting all casual, then slouched back in his chair and grinned at her. And waggled his eyebrows.

"Lance!"

It probably wasn't the smartest idea to get his mother worked up over nothing. But Lance felt a rare spark of playfulness and he couldn't help milking it.

"Not a thing special happened today," he said with utter falseness.

His mother twitched her nose and gave him her most dignified *hmph!*

*　　　　*　　　　*

Tim stood before the seed trays he'd prepared and took a deep breath. This was it. Time to slice open the fruits of his labor and see what happened.

He'd spent the last three days getting the greenhouse in working condition. The place had been filled with spiders, mice, desiccated plants, stacks of dirty pots, and a layer of dust so thick he'd had to wear a bandana over his mouth as he swept it out.

He'd patched some cracked windows, repaired a table leg, and bought a frugal list of planting supplies in Fresno.

And now he had a greenhouse. It wasn't much to look at, and it was pathetically understocked. But it got excellent light from sunup to three pm when the long shadows of the pines reached out to touch the glass. And it was his.

Taking a knife, he carefully sliced open one of the rose hips from bag '*A*' and shook out the seeds, being careful not to damage them. *A* was a cross of Wild Blue Yonder and Nostalgia. He was relieved to see nearly a dozen nice, fat seeds inside. He picked up the fattest candidates, one at a time, with the tip of a wooden plant marker and carefully pushed each one down into a square inch of soil in the tray. He planted a whole tray of rose *A* seeds and then moved on to the next bag of rose hips.

He had twenty different sets of rose hips, each one from a new hybrid. He'd prepared them last September, carefully brushing together the anthers from a father rosebush and the pistols from the mother. And when the rose hips had grown, he'd harvested them and frozen them to mimic frost. There they had stayed, in his refrigerator in his little studio apartment above Marshall's garage, until the night he'd left Santa Barbara. And they'd only been there, in his apartment, because Marshall was too cheap to install a fridge in the company greenhouse.

And thank God he was. Because there was no way Tim could hybridize and grow new roses in six months, and the promise of the perfect new rose was all that stood between him and homelessness.

"Be beautiful," he whispered to the tiny germs of life now buried in the loamy soil. He misted the tops of the trays with a spray bottle and sent them good juju. "Be lovely and strong. And if just *one* of my purple-tipped-ivories could pan out, I'd be forever grateful."

There was nothing to do now but wait. He knew the odds. It might take two hundred hybrid tries to come up with one rose worth keeping, much less something award-winning and truly new. But he'd selected very good parents for these so maybe....

Well, there was nothing left to do but wait on the seedlings *and* fill up the greenhouse with hundreds of trays of other seedlings, much more common, ordinary ones he could hopefully use to start a modest produce business.

Tim bagged up the smaller seeds that hadn't made the cut and put them, and the remains of the rose hips, in a big stainless steel bowl. He turned to carry them back to the house and—

—saw a face looking at him through the greenhouse glass. He screamed and threw up his hands. The bowl went flying in a wobbly, panicked arc. It landed with an ear-killing clang.

Wait. He knew that face. It was the cop from the diner. The cop broke into a grin for a brief moment before he went back to his glower. But that moment was enough. Tim didn't appreciate being laughed at. He narrowed his eyes, strode to the door, and yanked it open.

"You scared the shit out of me!"

"Apologies, sir." The cop was all legal authority now. It was sunny, and he wore mirrored sunglasses. He looked like someone cosplaying Eric Estrada except, yeah, way cuter. Holy smokes. He had a sexy dark shadow of stubble on his square jaw, full lips, and a nose that was big but worked in his manly face. And how did anyone even have a body like that? The guy was all compact muscle with a non-existent stomach and nicely defined quads that showed under his tight uniform pants, and... and everything.

Tim's righteous anger vaporized in a flush of nervousness he felt down to his toes. "Okay," he said lamely.

"This a greenhouse?" The cop asked politely, only it wasn't really polite at all. He took a step toward Tim, as if he wanted to

34

push past him and go inside. That would be necessary because Tim was standing in the doorway. He looked over his shoulder and realized there were rose hips all over the floor where the bowl had dumped out. *Oh, shit.*

"No!" Tim said loudly. He stepped out and closed the greenhouse door firmly behind him. "I have... um.... That is, it's a, uh, sterile environment. I can't have anyone in there right now. Sorry."

The cop very deliberately looked Tim up and down, and his nostrils flared as he sniffed. Even with the sunglasses blocking the man's eyes, Tim could read the look. He was disheveled, covered with dust and dirt from all his cleaning and probably stunk too. *Sterile? Why don't you pull the other one.*

"Hey! I'm thirsty. You thirsty? Wanna drink? Something? Want something to drink? I have water. No, that's boring. Coffee? Do you like coffee? 'Cause some people don't. I don't have any beer or anything. Not that you would care if I did. I'm over twenty-one. And it's legal if it's in a house. I mean, not an open bottle in a car. Not that you *would* drink beer on duty. I'm sure you would never do that, Officer."

Tim clapped a hand over his own mouth.

The cop took off his glasses and stared at Tim as if the

35

sunglasses might be responsible for his apparent lunacy.

Wow. Blue. Those eyes were seriously, seriously bright blue. Like the blue of the sky when it's really deep on a perfect fall day. And *man*, did the guy know how to stare with those orbs or what? Tim had never met anyone who could stare like that, like he was reaching right down inside you and poking around in the cobwebs in your darkest corners. Tim shivered.

The cop took one last greedy peek into the greenhouse and then took a step toward Tim. "All right. Coffee. Let's go." He crowded into Tim until Tim had no choice but to move toward the house. *Okay, okay. Geez. Personal space, buddy.*

"Sure!" Tim said lightly, and with the guy dogging his heels the entire way, he made it to the house.

*   *   *

Lance was starting to realize that the guy, T-Timothy, had two vocal speeds—monosyllabic and hyperdrive. He resorted to the former as he led Lance to the house, let them inside, and started fussing with coffee stuff in the kitchen. He dropped a cup, the cheap white ceramic shattering into a zillion pieces. Then he fumbled with the coffee filters like they were a hot potato. Lance watched, not saying a word and determined not to find it endearing. At all.

He wandered a bit while the coffee brewed, looking at everything. Not that there was much to see. The old furniture obviously belonged to the cabin, and there was little of the current inhabitant in sight other than a row of books in the otherwise empty bookcase. Lance studied the titles. They were gardening and plant books, a few heavy-looking texts on plant biology. There was nothing on growing pot. But even this guy wouldn't have a book like that sitting out where anyone could see it. There was no smell of marijuana in the cabin either, or on the boy today. Lance was sure he hadn't imagined it.

He was hardly being subtle in his interest, but then, he didn't want to be. He wanted to send a message loud and clear. *Whatever nefarious thing you're planning out here, you won't get away with it, not with me around.* That business out at the greenhouse? The way Timothy had panicked at the idea of Lance going in there and maybe getting an eyeful of what he was planting? Lance hadn't liked that one bit. The guy was up to something.

Normally, Lance could trust his gut instinct about people,

but Timothy was confusing. On the one hand, Lance knew damn well he was lying and hiding things. But on the other hand, he appeared to be naive and dorky, innocent in a way that made Lance's inner dog wag its tail. But it was an act—had to be. Lance couldn't let himself fall for it.

He wandered back into the kitchen as Timothy poured the coffee. Lance held his breath, but nothing further was spilled, broken, or disastrously fumbled.

"Did you buy this place?" Lance asked casually.

"Me? Hardly." The guy gave a sad little laugh.

"Renting?"

"Cream? Well, milk really. Two percent. Sorry. I don't have sugar. I have honey, but it has some crystally bits in it. Not that those will hurt you. I don't think. Not many people like honey in their coffee, though. Even, you know, fresh honey. Although people use it for tea. So you'd figure, coffee! Especially if you like sugar and there isn't any. But then, most people probably have sugar around."

Lance let Timothy spew on for a bit. He was either a really bad liar or a brilliant one.

Timothy finally ran out of words and looked at Lance

38

expectantly, still holding his cup.

"Black," Lance said, taking the cup.

"Oh." Timothy blushed.

If the guy thought he could distract Lance, *Lance*, for God's sake, he was mistaken. "So. You renting this place?"

"Um. Sort of. Yeah."

"From....?"

"Linda Fitzgibbons," Timothy said smoothly, but he blushed harder.

Lance had looked up the land owner before he'd come out here, so he knew Timothy was telling the truth. At least that showed he probably wasn't a squatter. From what Lance was able to tell, the Fitzgibbons had owned this property on Broad Eagle Drive for twenty-two years, but they used it as a vacation home and rarely even that. Lance couldn't recall their faces, and he knew everyone around here.

"Yeah? What's she charge for a place like this?" Lance sipped his coffee. It was surprisingly good.

"Well... n-nothing right now. It's sort of..." Timothy trailed off warily.

39

"Barter arrangement?" Lance suggested.

"Yeah!" Timothy brightened.

"She gets some of your profits?"

"Exactly!" Timothy smiled as if relieved not to have to explain it. Lance just stared at him. Timothy's smile faltered. "Or... um... what?"

Lance straightened up and put down the coffee cup very deliberately. He put one hand on his hip near his gun. "What are you planning to grow here, Mr. Traynor?"

For a second, Timothy looked afraid. Then he seemed to grow a backbone—or maybe drop the pretense of not having one.

He straightened up tall, and his face grew angry and defensively shuttered. "Pardon me, Officer Beaufort, but I don't see how that's any of your business. I've tried to be civil. But you—"

"Sheriff Beaufort."

"Wh-what?" Timothy glanced at the badge on Lance's jacket, confused. "It says 'Sheriff', but I thought that just meant 'Sheriff's Department'. Like—"

"*I* am the Sheriff," Lance interrupted again. "Sheriff Lance Beaufort."

Timothy looked more confused than impressed. "Well... what's the sheriff doing harassing me? I'm nobody!" Timothy huffed a strange little laugh, but there was still a touch of fear lurking in those eyes.

"It's a simple question. What are you planning to grow here, Mr. Traynor?" Lance took one step closer, crowding the man.

"None of your business, Sheriff Beaufort." Timothy held his ground and, surprisingly, met Lance's stare. He tilted his chin up stubbornly for good measure.

There was a weird frisson as Timothy's hazel eyes stared challengingly into Lance's, a bubbling energy at the base of Lance's spine and a *rat a tat tat* rhythm that tripped through his heart like a tap dancer crossing the stage. He wasn't used to being defied and denied. When Lance asked people to jump around here, they bounced like freaking Ping-Pong balls.

Timothy's eyes might be defiant, but his lower lip trembled. Lance stared at it.

"I have to get back to work," Timothy said abruptly. "If

you want to visit me again, maybe you can get a warrant?"

Lance looked back up into Timothy's eyes, said nothing.

"And you might want to work on your town's welcoming committee. Maybe invite a few little old ladies to participate. Tell them I want my fucking fruit basket."

And with that, Timothy Traynor marched to the front door and held it open pointedly.

~3~

Struck Dumb

"MRS. FITZGIBONS? This is Sheriff Beaufort in Mad Creek."

It'd been a few days since Lance had been thrown out on his ear by Timothy Traynor. He'd been busy. There'd been a battalion of bad-news bikers who stopped in town and had to be encouraged to go spread their leathery charms elsewhere. He and Deputy Smith had searched the neighboring woods for two hikers who had vanished from the Ansel Adams Wilderness. It was unlikely they'd made it this far south, but they'd looked anyway. Fortunately, the hikers had finally been found by another search party near Alpine Lakes. Lance had to attend the city board meeting and give a report. And Lance's mother had practically dragged him by the scruff of his neck to the McGurvers to see baby Samantha.

She was very cute. And so warm to hold. Fine. Whatever.

But no matter what Lance had been doing, a certain young man with floppy brown hair—*the color of dark straw maybe*—never completely left his mind.

Lance had a sixth sense about these sorts of things, and he was still feeling itchy about Timothy. Either the guy was trouble or he was *in* trouble. Hell, from what Lance had seen of Timothy Traynor, it could easily be both at the same time.

Mrs. Fitzgibbons's voice on the other end of the phone line sounded alarmed. "Sheriff? What can I do for you? Is everything all right?"

"Fine, fine. Just a routine call. You're renting out your Mad Creek cabin at the moment?"

"Well… yes. Yes, I am."

"I just wanted to make sure you knew someone was staying there."

"Well, of course I know."

"Good. Would you mind giving me the name of your tenant?"

Lance waited, tapping the paper on his desk with the tip of his pen.

"I suppose…. You're sure everything's all right?"

"It's fine, Mrs. Fitzgibbons. It's just when we have a property like this that's normally empty, we like to make sure we don't get people taking advantage."

"I see. Well, it isn't empty *now*. I suspect it'll be good for the place. His name's Tim. Tim Weston. Very nice boy."

Ah.

"Is he from this area?" Lance asked.

"No, I met him here. I mean, where we currently reside." Mrs. Fitzgibbons was being coy and was starting to sound suspicious. Once more into the breach.

"I see. Do you know if he has plans to do anything with the property? Repairs? Clearing land?"

There was silence on the other end of the line. "I don't know. He can do whatever he likes as far as I'm concerned." There was a false note in her voice.

"Right. Well thank you for your time, Mrs. Fitzgibbons. I appreciate the info."

Leesa came in with some bills that needed to be signed, and

Lance's deputy, Charlie Smith, came in to shoot the shit. Charlie was descended from bloodhounds. He was a gifted tracker and incredibly tenacious when trouble came down, but he wasn't the brightest pup in the litter. When Lance was alone again, the itch inside was bigger and more irritating than ever. Timothy had lied about his name. Lance wasn't exactly surprised. The question was: why? Lance couldn't let it go. He hesitated, then picked up the phone and called Sam Miller at District Headquarters in Fresno. Lance usually tried to keep dealings with Fresno as light as possible, preferring Mad Creek to stay off the radar. But they had resources he didn't.

"I need a background check on a Tim Weston aka Timothy Traynor recently of Santa Barbara." Mrs. Fitzgibbons might have been coy, but her property deed was in the system along with her current address.

"Sure. What are you looking for?" Sam asked.

Lance told Sam about his suspicions, and Sam promised to run the check right away. Then Sam told him more horror stories about the gang activity they'd seen in Fresno. It was a gateway to the California mountains and hearing about the increased activity there did nothing to soothe Lance's nerves.

Even before he'd hung up with Sam, Lance knew he was

prepared to go further to find out what Tim Weston was up to.

Much further.

*   *   *

Tim coaxed Bessy up the road that led from downtown Mad Creek to the cabin. He'd had to run to Fresno for more supplies, and it had first rained, then snowed, all the way home. The late season flurries would no doubt be melted by noon tomorrow, but it was still awesome. The road was steep, though, and Tim knew one of these days Bessy would peter out halfway up, the little engine that couldn't. Luckily she climbed gamely on, despite the white stuff on the road.

He'd bought another two dozen of the cheapest plastic seed trays they had at the gardening center. They'd have mold problems over the long-term, but they were good enough for his first season. And he'd hit Costco and loaded up on mac and cheese and canned tuna too. The prices were way better than anything at the small grocery store in Mad Creek.

Mad Creek. The place was starting to feel like home. He liked it. He'd lived in Southern California all his life, never been

47

anywhere else. But despite the fact that most of his cultural references to the woods came from films like *Friday the 13th* and *In the Woods No One Can Hear You Being Disemboweled* he actually found the mountains quite peaceful. He loved the nip to the air that allowed him to wear his old canvas jacket. He liked that the air smelled of green and growing things rather than sun and sand. And he adored the weather. He was so used to 70 and sunny that any sort of weather at all was a rare treat. It had been mostly cloudy and cool since he'd arrived. And now snow! Heaven!

He liked everything about Mad Creek, except, maybe, for Sheriff Beaufort. Tim still couldn't believe he'd stood up to the man the other day. But he'd been pushed far enough. After his dad, and then what'd happened with Marshall, he'd promised himself he wouldn't be so gullible, wouldn't be a pushover anymore. It was the only way he could live with himself. The sheriff might be way hot, but he was obviously the kind of dickhead who got off on power trips. He liked to throw his weight around. Well, he had no grounds to be on Linda's property, and Tim didn't have to put up with that. He wasn't doing anything wrong.

Okay, maybe he was doing something a little wrong. Those

rose hips had technically been the property of Roots of Life since Tim's stupid employee contract gave the company full rights to *everything* he did or thought or shat while he'd worked there, even though he'd grafted those hybrids at home. But Marshall had already made enough money off Tim's creations, and he didn't even *know* about the rose hips.

Tim hoped.

Besides, he had no choice but to use them. Starting from scratch was one thing, but roses... roses took time and care and love. A lot of love.

It started snowing harder, and the window defroster was having a hell of a time keeping up. Like Tim, Bessy had never had to deal with this kind of weather. Maybe the snow wasn't all that wonderful, not when you were outside in the stuff. Fortunately, he was almost home. He could see the light on the cabin porch now. He misjudged the swing into the driveway and the truck hit a massive pot hole and lurched jarringly downward. Tim hit the gas hard hoping to pull the truck out of the hole and, just as he did, he saw a black dog trotting down his driveway— right toward him. The truck lurched forward, Tim screamed, hit the brakes, and—

There was a thump on the front side of the car and then a

49

doggy howl of pain.

Tim threw the truck into park, feeling like he was about to puke. "Oh, God, no. Please, no."

He jumped out of the driver's side and tore around the front of the truck. Lying there, in the muck and snow, was a black dog. It looked like some kind of large collie mix with long, shaggy black hair so thick the melting snow rolled right off it. He—definitely a he—was lying on his right side in the mud, his mouth open and tongue lolling. He waved a feeble paw in the air.

"Oh, buddy!" Tim got down on his hands and knees, not caring about the snow and mud. He started to reach out for the dog and then realized the dog might bite. And who could blame him if he did? If someone hit Tim with a truck, he'd bite them too.

"Um…. You okay? Of course you're not. Are you in pain? Is it your paw?" Tim's hand hovered in mid-air, afraid to get closer.

The dog opened his eyes. He had blue eyes—brilliant blue. He gave Tim a pathetic look. He didn't seem vicious.

Tim was nearly in tears. He tentatively put his hand on the dog's head and gave him what he hoped with a soothing pet.

"I'm so, so sorry! I tried to stop. Oh, you poor thing! I'll get help, don't worry."

The dog started to get up, but Tim pushed him back down with a *splat.* "No! Don't move. You could make it worse. Just stay there, okay? Please?"

This was horrible. Tim would never willingly hurt an animal, and he'd hit this one *with his truck.* True, he hadn't been going very fast, but the truck had really bounced out of that hole as he floored it. God knows what kind of damage he'd done to the dog.

He encouraged the dog to stay down as he petted it with one hand while the other fished his cell phone from a pocket.

Oh, shit. He had no idea where to find a vet in the area. He decided to try 911.

"Hey, sorry to bother you, but I was hoping you could help me find a vet?" He sounded barely in control, his voice thick. "I just hit a dog with my car. Mad Creek. Um... I'm not sure. He's conscious. And he's looking at me. Well, glaring really."

The dog was glaring, too. It looked pointedly at the half-frozen mud it was lying in and then shot doggy daggers at Tim. "Hang in there, buddy," Tim cooed. "I'm getting help."

The 911 operator was a dog lover, and she was all helpful and encouraging. "Don't move him, sweetie. There is a 24-hour animal emergency line for Mad Creek, and I'll connect you. Good luck! I hope he's okay."

The 24-hour animal emergency line for Mad Creek said they had an on-call vet and they would send him right out. The woman on the phone asked if he wanted her to alert the police too.

Before Tim could answer, the black dog gave off a set of annoyed-sounding barks. He struggled to get up again.

"Shhh, puppy! I don't know. Do you think I need to? Call the police? I didn't mean to hit him." Tim could just picture Sheriff Blowhard staring at him all disgusted because he'd hit a poor, defenseless dog. He'd probably cuff him and strip-search him before calling out the firing squad.

Strip-searched by Sheriff McHotty. Not really the time to be thinking about that.

The woman on the line must have heard the guilt and fear in Tim's voice, because she tried to reassure him. "Of course you didn't! Tell you what, let's wait and see if Dr. McGurver thinks he needs to bother the police. Okay? He should be there soon."

Tim gushed his thanks and put his phone away. With his hands and attention free, he got down on all fours to be closer to the dog. The dog seemed to relax too, and lay down flat in the mud, panting and lifting that one paw in the air with a whine. The snow on the dog's thick coat melted and ran off in streams as Tim petted him gently, trying to see if he could find any blood or obvious injuries. He was a beautiful animal. He had a regal air about him. Tim would feel awful if he'd killed a creature like this. He could feel heat on his face and knew it was tears.

"Please be okay," Tim whispered to the dog.

Right then it seemed like the only thing that mattered.

*　　　　　*　　　　　*

Lance was beginning to feel really bad about this. The concept had been simple—pretend to be mildly hurt by Tim's truck and get inside the house overnight on sympathy. He figured twenty-four hours max on the 'inside', and he'd be able to see once and for all what Timothy Traynor aka Tim Weston was really up to.

No, it wasn't exactly above board. But the guy was hiding

something, and Lance figured the higher good was protecting his community. Once he'd gotten the idea, it had been hard to dislodge it. And anyway, he could always abort if things went wrong. Right? And no one would ever know he'd stooped so low.

But now, seeing the stricken look on the guy's face, the tears that trembled on his lashes, the way he looked so miserable, sodden and cold in the snow, and the way he touched Lance's pelt so gently, murmuring apologies and promises so… so….

So ridiculously inane.

Damn! Who would have thought the guy would be such a pushover for a strange dog?

Lance struggled to get up again. This time he was determined to show Tim he wasn't seriously hurt. He couldn't bear the guy's guilt any longer. If it meant Lance could forget being taken in for the night, so be it. This was just cruel.

The lights of a car pulled into the driveway. It was Bill McGurver. Damn it.

Bill jumped out of his vehicle and came running. Lance was still in the mud, pinned by the glare of the old truck's headlights. He raised his paw and gave a weak whine as Bill dropped to his knees.

Bill stared at him, horrified. "Lance? Oh my God, are you all right?"

"Do you know this dog?" Tim said anxiously. "I'm so sorry! I was just coming up my driveway and I hit a pothole and suddenly he was right there! I think maybe the front of my truck got him. Please tell me he'll be okay!"

Lance narrowed his eyes at Bill. *Keep your mouth shut.*

"Um..." Bill spluttered. Wet, clumpy snow built up on the hood of his anorak as he stared at Lance in confusion. "I meant... Wow, what a *chance* you took, handling a strange dog like this. Mr...?"

"I'm Tim. I couldn't just let him lie here hurt! He keeps holding up his paw." Tim's voice was all shaky, and he was petting Lance's coat compulsively. His hands were warm, which was a little odd. Given how thick Lance's pelt was, he wouldn't have expected to feel body heat like that. But then again, he was very cold and wet. "Can you help him, Doctor? Please?"

Dont give me away. Lance ordered Bill with his eyes.

"Let's get him inside where it's warm," Bill said decisively.

"Is it okay to move him? What if he has internal injuries?"

"Best check." Bill ran his hands over Lance's back and hind legs, obviously unsure what he was dealing with and how badly Lance was actually hurt. He glanced into Lance's eyes, and Lance shook his head a fraction and then held up his left paw with a whine any dog worth his salt—or a human who lived with one, like Bill—would know was fake.

Bill grimaced and took the paw, feeling around it carefully. He gave Lance a disapproving look. "I think it's fine to move him into the house. And I don't know about you, but I've had enough of this snow."

"Okay." Tim sounded relieved. "He'll probably feel better where it's warm."

Lance limped convincingly to the cabin, whining every time he put weight on his paw.

"Do you have any old towels?" Bill asked when they were all standing, dripping, in the cabin's living room.

"Yeah, there's a whole closet of 'em." Tim leaned down to look into Lance's eyes with warm concern and stroked his head. "I'll be right back, buddy. Okay?"

Lance narrowed his eyes. *Well, duh.*

"He seems really… I dunno… intelligent for a dog," Tim said with admiration.

"You think so?" Bill said dryly. "I'd have thought it was unaccountably stupid to *run out in front of a truck*, and *way out here* of all places."

"Maybe he was lost. I need to get him dry." Tim raced off as if he were going after life-saving plasma or maybe a heart to transplant instead of towels.

Bill squatted down and spoke to Lance in an urgent hush. "What are you doing out here? What happened?"

Lance gave a sharp bark. *I know what I'm doing.*

Bill frowned, but he examined Lance's paw. "Where did he hit you? Your paw doesn't seem to be swollen."

Lance did the best doggy eye roll he could summon.

"So you're not hurt? At all?" Bill felt around Lance's paw. The pressure of his touch increased along with his impatience.

Lance panted and sighed.

"Fine. I don't know what you were doing out here *like this*, but you can ride back to town with me."

Lance let Bill know what he thought about that idea.

"What happened?" Tim came rushing in with a Chinese laundry's worth of towels in his arms. He dumped them on the floor and dropped to his knees. "Why's he barking like that? Is he in pain?"

"No, that's his imperious bark. He's telling me a thing or two," Bill said with a huff.

Bill got to his feet and opened up his medical backpack. "Let's see. A nice big bandage for that paw, I think."

"Is he going to be okay? Can I dry him off now? Do you know whose dog this is? I don't see a collar. What kind of dog is he? He seems friendly enough, don't you think?"

"Yes. Yes. No. And *no*. I'm not sure what breed he is other than a stubborn one." Bill always had been a smart ass.

"Sorry. I ask too many questions, huh? Yes, he's going to be okay? Really?"

"He's going to be fine. Or as fine as he's ever been anyway."

Bill knelt down with a bundle of white gauze in one hand

and bright fluorescent pink bandage wrap in the other. *Bastard.*

"You don't think he has any internal bleeding or anything?" Tim insisted worriedly as Bill wrapped up Lance's paw.

Bill stopped wrapping and looked at Tim, his face softening. He put a hand on Tim's shoulder. "Hey, Tim. He's fine. And I'm sure whatever happened was not your fault. Okay? Just breathe."

Tim did, literally, heaving a deep breath and letting it out. He got a bit of color back into his cheeks. Lance's guilt reasserted itself. As if making Tim feel wretched wasn't bad enough, he'd never live this down with Bill.

God, please don't let him tell my mother.

"You can dry him off now," Bill said as he finished up the hideous pink sausage. He'd wrapped up Lance's paw from nail to torso. *Jerk.*

Tim all but attacked Lance with the largest, fluffiest towel in the pile. Lance bore it with all the dignity he could muster whilst wearing one pink leg.

"Gah, he's covered in mud!"

"He is, isn't he?" Bill got a glint in his eye that Lance

59

didn't care for at all. "Why don't you give him a bath? A warm one. With lots of shampooing."

Lance growled a warning, which was ignored.

"Could I?" Tim sounded like he'd just been offered a trip to Disneyland.

"I rather think you should," said Bill seriously.

"What about his bandage?"

"Oh, that wrap is waterproof. It'll be fine. I wouldn't soak it, though. See if you can get him to hold it up the entire time."

Lance's warning growl deepened.

But Tim looked so hopeful. He gently wiped Lance's face with the towel. "Did you say earlier that you *do* know him? He's not wearing a collar. He must belong to someone, though, because he's in beautiful condition."

Bill snorted. "I know all the dogs in this area, Tim. And I'm pretty sure this dog belongs to *nobody*."

Tim looked unabashedly pleased. "If I... if I wanted to keep him. You know, to make up for hitting him and everything, do I need to get a dog license or register somewhere?" There was a hitch of excitement in his voice. "Would you like that, buddy?

Would you?"

Bill gave a low chuckle. "You don't need a license, but I think if you want to keep this one around, you'll have to convince *him* of that. Isn't that right, puppy?" Bill gushed in a most undignified voice and rubbed Lance's ears.

Lance growled louder this time.

"Hey, be nice!" Tim wrapped a proprietary arm around Lance's shoulders as if prepared to hold him back. As if he could. "Maybe he smells other dogs on you. That could feel threatening to him."

Bill snorted. "I'm sure that's it. Well, that about does it. Remember—long, hot bath. Oh, and I wouldn't give him anything but water at least until morning if not for twenty-four hours."

"*Errrr,*" said Lance.

"Okay, um, what do I owe you?" Tim sounded worried as Bill headed for the door with his backpack. "I mean, I know it's off-hours and it's dark and snowing and everything. And I'm so grateful he's all right...."

Don't take his money, Lance thought, knowing the guy had very little. If Bill charged him, he'd have to pay the boy back somehow.

"Don't worry about it. It was on my way home. And it was worth it to be able to see such a nice dog so well cared for."

"Really? That's super generous of you."

Bill opened the door. The snow was still coming down like wet cotton. Bill leaned in to speak in Tim's ear. But Lance's hearing was very good, and he heard it all the same.

"Be sure to give him lots of hugs and pets. It'll help him over the shock," Bill whispered.

Lance could hear him laughing all the way to his car.

~4~
A Boy's Best Friend

LANCE THOUGHT about trying to make a break for it. But after all he'd put Tim Traynor-aka-Weston through, if he didn't finish the job now, he really would be an utter bastard. He tried refusing to cooperate on the bath thing, but that wasn't as easy as it sounded.

"Please, buddy? Your coat is all muddy, and that can't feel good. A nice bath will make you feel so much better." The soothing-pleading words were accompanied by big, soulful eyes and those ever-present tender strokes of his fur. Lance heaved a sigh. Something about Tim made Lance want to please him. Probably he just felt sorry for the guy. And guilt. Yes, it was definitely guilt.

What did you expect? You're pretending to be a dog, so you have to be a dog. Get over it.

In truth, Lance was disgustingly filthy, thanks to Tim pushing him down in the cold mud. But he'd never bathed in dog form, much less let a *human* bathe him. That was just... humiliating. What he wanted was to shift back into his human form and have a nice, long, hot shower. But that wasn't going to happen if he was going to stick around till Tim fell asleep.

Somehow, Lance found himself being led, limping on his pink leg, into the bathroom. Tim shut the bathroom door. The air in there was hazy with the steam from a bathtub full of hot water.

"I would have added bubble bath, but I was worried it might irritate your skin." Tim ran his hand through the bath water, testing the temperature. Lance looked at the steamy water and looked at Tim.

Tim made no move to force Lance into the tub. He pulled off his own shirt, tugging the long-sleeved T-shirt over his head to reveal a thin frame with surprisingly broad shoulders, and then knelt by the tub. Lance looked away, surprised by the way Tim's naked chest felt too intimate, almost as if he was an attractive woman. Then again, Tim's skin looked really soft and he did smell awfully good.

Lance sank down into a sit and plopped his pink pole of a leg down in front of him. He panted with anxiety. His dog was uneasy. The door was closed, and he was trapped in there. Trapped with a half-naked Tim. Tim, who was trying very hard to take care of him. The dog didn't want to hurt Tim, which meant he was going to have to do whatever Tim wanted.

"I'm going to get soaking wet, I suppose. It doesn't matter. Come on, buddy. You need this. You'll feel so much better with all that mud out of your fur."

Lance heaved a long, heartfelt sigh. Tim moved toward him, apparently intent on picking Lance up. Well, if this had to happen, at least Lance could retain some dignity. He pulled away and jumped into the tub himself. It wasn't the most graceful maneuver he'd ever made, with his front left paw stiff and foreign feeling, and water went everywhere.

Tim laughed. The sound sparkled off the bathroom tiles. "Okay, that works. Holy cow." He threw some towels on the floor to sop up the spill and knelt beside the tub. "Let's put your leg up here. Come on." He gently tugged Lance's pink leg up to rest on the edge of the tub. Now it was pink and wet. Lovely. But Tim dried it off carefully with a towel and that pink wrap was probably made out of alien space plastic or something, because it looked like it had never seen a drop of water in its life.

Tim had his hands on Lance—one on the pink leg and one

on the opposite shoulder. He stared as he knelt by the tub. He was wearing a funny little smile.

"You have the biggest, bluest, most beautifulest eyes ever, do you know that?" He was using the kind of voice his mother used when she talked to baby Samantha.

Lance huffed.

"Wanna know something? I've never had a dog before. I always wanted one, but my mom didn't want one in the house." Tim stroked Lance's temple, right by his ear. The warm water did feel good after the cold and the snow. Between that and the steam and Tim's rumbly voice, it was hard not to relax. The fingers on his temple felt so good, like they were soothing away a headache he didn't know he had. And he hadn't noticed before, but Tim had a very deep voice. Maybe he'd never noticed it because Tim had always been nervous in the presence of Lance, the cop. Lance, the dog, really liked the tone of it, the way its low register tickled his ears, and the loving cadence to it.

Yeah, he'd be real loving if he knew who you were.

"And then when I worked for the nursery, I lived above the owner's garage, and he wouldn't let me have any pets there either! What a meany, huh?" Tim took Lance's head in both hands and looked into his eyes. "We don't like Marshall, do we?

66

No we don't!"

Lance barked in agreement. He wasn't easily won over by humans in any case, so not liking this Marshall wasn't much of a stretch.

"Probably for the best, though, since I spent most of my time working in the greenhouse. Not much of a life for a dog." Tim poured shampoo into the palm of his hand and began to work it into Lance's fur. "Hope this is okay. I don't have any dog shampoo. Guess I'll have to pick some up, huh?"

Lance was trying to focus on the tidbits of information Tim was dropping—nursery, greenhouse, Marshall—and not on Tim's hands, but it was hard. The way they worked over his soapy fur, the nails lightly scratching, felt incredible. His eyes went half-lidded and his tongue lolled out. Christ. No wonder his mother always wanted a spa trip for her birthday. Lance couldn't remember the last time he'd been pampered in anything by anyone. He didn't need things like that. Never allowed himself the luxury.

"But now that we live out here, you can run around in the yard while I work. That'll be okay, won't it? I'll leave the greenhouse door open so you can come in and keep me company whenever you get bored."

Right there. That little… Ah. Lance gave a whimper as Tim's lovely scrubbing fingers moved over an itchy place. What was Tim saying? Open access to the greenhouse. That would be good.

Not that Lance planned on sticking around. Twenty-four hours. In and out.

Tim's long, strong fingers massaged over Lance's ribs. "You're not too skinny. That's good. But that means you must belong to someone, though, huh? No matter what Dr. McGurver said."

Lance cracked his eyes open to look at Tim. He looked simultaneously hopeful and sad. "I know I'd go crazy if I lost a dog like you, so I guess I have to at least look for your owners." He pulled a glass off the counter and used it to rinse Lance off. The water sent soap streaming down Lance's black fur in warm waves. "But I'm not going to look *that* hard. And if no one is missing a dog, would you like to live here with me?"

Tim's hand ran over Lance's clean fur, squeezing out some of the water. "I'm probably not your best choice of an owner, honestly. I'm not even sure if I'll have a home six months from now. You see, I'm growing a bunch of stuff I hope to sell in the summer. But what if I can't make a living at it? And then there's the rose I promised Linda." Tim sighed.

Stuff? What stuff? Rose? What rose?

"But I'll do the best I can by you. I promise." Tim, now soaking wet himself, helped Lance out of the tub and onto some dry towels he'd put on the bathroom floor. Then he proceeded to rub Lance all over with more dry towels. Lance really wanted to shake to dislodge the water, but he refrained, knowing he'd get it everywhere. And the sensation of Tim rubbing him briskly was... sufficient.

Tim got the worst of the water off Lance. But instead of moving away, he put his arms around Lance and hugged him. There they sat—Lance sitting on his hind legs and Tim with his long legs and damp jeans sitting cross-legged right in front of him, leaning forward and hugging him, the towel still wrapped over Lance's back. Tim's face was over Lance's shoulder, so he couldn't see his expression, but he felt something, something open and hot and vulnerable pouring off the young man. Lance trembled. It was so private. He should pull away, this was taking advantage in a way he hadn't anticipated. But he didn't move.

"I'm so glad you're all right. I would've hated myself if you'd been badly hurt."

Oh, God.

69

Tim pulled back and smiled brightly. "Now what should I call you? I bet you don't want to get stuck with 'Buddy', huh?"

Nothing. No name. That's fine. Seriously.

Tim looked thoughtful. "What about Chance? Dr. McGurver said I'd taken a *chance* touching you. And I guess you are a chance at something new for me. Maybe I'm a chance for you too. What do you think, Chance? Do you like it?"

Lance plopped his head on Tim's shoulder with a sigh. He was in so much trouble.

*   *   *

After the bath, Tim changed into flannel PJ bottoms and a T-shirt and made himself a sandwich. He ate it while they sat on the couch and watched *Twilight Zone*. Lance tried not to look at the sandwich, but he was feeling more than a little peckish and his dog instincts were clearly interested—warm, safe, *food*. The doggie trifecta. Yes, food would be lovely right about then.

Tim pouted out his lip. "I'm sorry, Chance, but I can't give you anything. Doctor's orders. We'll get you a nice big breakfast, though, okay? Do you like eggs? I picked up a dozen

70

in Fresno, and I'll scramble you three as soon as we get up. Maybe some toast too. Which reminds me. I'll have to run out and get some dog food tomorrow."

Lance lay down on the couch with a grumble and closed his eyes so he couldn't see the food. Tim petted his back with one hand while he ate. Lance's fur felt soft and clean from the bath. He wondered idly if he should try that shampoo and if his human hair would feel this good if he used it.

While Tim munched, occasionally Lance would open his eyes and peek at the TV. He hadn't watched *Twilight Zone* in years. He'd forgotten that he liked it.

There were a lot of things Lance hadn't done in years, he realized. And plenty that he'd never done at all.

Lance loved the dog part of his nature. It was happy, good-natured, loyal, and protective of those he cared about. In his experience, he preferred quickened to humans any day. But despite this, he rarely shifted into his animal form. He'd been born with it, a fourth genner. As a kid, he'd been reluctant to shift that first time, afraid of losing himself, of losing control. But finally his friends had goaded him into it when he was twelve. And all through high school, he'd worn his animal form whenever he could. It felt great to run in the woods with his friends, to wrestle and play. He'd always been a serious boy, and becoming a dog let him experience being playful and carefree for the first time in his life.

But then he grew up. His dad was the sheriff, and Lance got a job with the department. He was determined to prove he was there because he deserved to be, and not just because he was his father's son. He had big footsteps to fill. Everyone respected Sheriff Clifford Beaufort. The time to play had gotten harder and harder to find. Others in the community had a regular 'howl at the moon night' once a month, running in the mountains just for the joy of it.

And exercise, his mother always insisted. *It's good for you to use those muscles, to shift back and forth. Keeps you young and sharp! Your dog needs to play.*

Lance always insisted he got plenty of exercise on the job. And what if an emergency came up while he was off romping around in his fur? It's not like he could carry his cell phone. Since his dad's passing, leaving the ship unattended even for a moment was not an option.

But being in his dog form was one thing. This was something else entirely. Lance had never, ever pretended to actually *be* a dog with a full-blooded human. He'd never been on

72

the receiving end of petting hands, hugs, and endearments, and, for god's sake, a bath! He should be horrified at the very idea. But, in his dog form, it was all strangely... okay. In fact, if he was honest with himself, it felt disturbingly comfortable and distressingly nice. It was like sinking into a warm, fluffy bed.

No wonder some of the newly quickened decided to go back to living full-time as a dog. It wasn't something the community approved of. Understood—yes. Their dog nature still had a strong pull to be with humans. With the right human, being a dog full-time was a very easy path in life. But Lance always found such behavior a complete and inexcusable cop-out. The gift of the spark was just that—a tremendous gift. To ignore the fact that you could think and reason and talk, that you could stand on your own two legs and take care of yourself and others, could be an agent in the human world, was to spit in the face of that gift. He'd never understood how anyone could make that choice.

And how frightening it was, too. Living as a dog meant not having control. Someone else decided everything for you, held your life in their hands. No thank you.

Lance himself had never felt much of a pull to be with a specific human being. Never before. But now, the dog side of his nature felt a stab of longing for the man sitting next to him. And that gave his human side a rush of pure fear. He jumped down off the couch.

"Chance? What is it, bud? You need to go out?"

Tim went to the door and opened it, but Lance just looked out at the snow with zero interest, and back up at Tim. Tim was appealing like this—in his pajamas, relaxed, and open. He seemed... nice. Cute. *Warm.* And so different than the nervous, stumbling, defensive guy Lance had met while wearing his uniform. He wondered if Tim was ever able to show this side of himself to other people.

But... no. Lance refused to be drawn to Tim, either as a dog or a man. That wasn't the plan. He limped to the corner of the room and lay down, curled up facing the wall.

Tim came over and scratched Lance's ears. "Are you tired? You can lay on the couch with me and sleep."

But Lance ignored the words, the slight hurt in Tim's voice, and the urge inside himself to do what Tim wanted, to take the comfort offered. Lance closed his eyes.

"It's okay. It's been a big night, huh? It'll take time for us to get used to each other."

Tim went into the hall and came back with a big comforter, which he doubled up and put next to Lance. "There you go. That'll be a little more comfortable than the floor at least."

When Tim went back to the couch, Lance crawled onto the comforter, curled up, and went to sleep.

~5~

Bring Me A Bone

LANCE WOKE up before dawn. He padded down the hall and looked in on Tim to make sure he was asleep. Tim was tucked into his bed on his stomach, his arm wrapped around a pillow, a cute patch of drool by his mouth. He'd left the bedroom door open. For Chance?

Lance, still a dog, poked around the house but didn't find anything new. Tim didn't seem to have that many personal belongings in the place. And there was no scent of smoke of the legal or illegal variety. Next, Lance went out to the greenhouse. It took him an annoying ten minutes of worrying at the pink bandage on his leg with his teeth to get it off so he could shift back to his human form. He let himself inside the greenhouse, planning to search it. Which made him nervous. Tim coming out to the greenhouse at dawn to find the Mad Creek sheriff, naked, was not a good scenario. He had no idea if Tim was an early riser.

Lance felt rushed and still a little out of it after having spent the night in dog form. The greenhouse was tidy, and he didn't find anything to confirm or refute his suspicions. There were bags of fertilizer, potting soil, and a spare little arrangement of older tools. Mainly, there were a whole lot of big trays with little individual pockets filled with dirt. Some of the trays were marked simply '*A*' or '*B*'. Others had strange names like 'C-GHST' or 'P-GSN', which meant nothing to Lance. Whatever Tim had planted, it hadn't sprouted yet. But surely that had to happen soon. A week at most, right? He'd have to hit Google when he got to the office to see how long seeds took to germinate.

Lance gave up, too worried about getting caught to linger. He shifted back into his dog and ran home, arriving at first light. He took a shower and got dressed in his uniform, and was back on the road by seven a.m.

* * *

Lance wove his way up the mountain, appreciating the

view on his right as the trees dropped away. Most of last night's snow was already gone, but there was still a layer of white in the shady spots. A driveway came into view, and he pulled his police cruiser into it cautiously, flashing his lights. Roman Charsguard was understood to be a badass, and not one to welcome strangers on his land. When Lance pulled up at the small house in the woods, Roman was on the porch, standing in military rest. His eyes followed Lance's every move. He looked relaxed, but Lance was fairly certain he had a weapon on him somewhere. Maybe several.

Lance studied the situation, then got out of the car. He rested his hands on the hood of the cruiser where Roman could see them. He looked at Roman's shoulder rather than meeting his gaze which Roman might take as a challenge.

"Morning, Roman."

There was half a tick, then Roman stepped out of his pose, and came toward Lance, holding out his hand. "Sheriff Beaufort. Nice to see you."

Lance shook his hand. "Call me Lance, please."

"Lance," said Roman, stiffly as if he preferred to be more formal.

Lance relaxed and assessed Roman quickly. He was a big man—six two and forcefully built. He was still relatively young and he looked healthy to Lance's eye, physically at least. Mentally was another matter.

"How you doing up here, Roman?"

"Very well, thank you, sir."

"Good. Good. Well. I wanted to see how you were. And also, I have something I wanted to get your opinion on, if you can spare the time."

Roman perked up, his shoulders going back and his eyes brightening. "I'm happy to be of service. Come inside. I have coffee on."

Lance had never been inside Roman's house, though Roman had moved to their community a little over a year ago. Lance had vetted him, of course. No quick ever moved to Mad Creek without Lance checking him or her out on paper, and his mother taking the often confused creature under her wing and essentially doing the same in her own inimitable way. Nothing got past Lily Beaufort.

Roman had been a military service dog, a highly trained German shepherd. No one knew the exact story of how he'd gotten the spark, or how and when he'd left the military and found his way to Mad Creek. He was a private man, tight-lipped and a little intimidating. Honestly, Lance wasn't sure what to make of him other than feeling fairly confident Roman was not a threat to their community, not least because Lily said so. In fact, she was always encouraging Lance to use Roman's talents to lessen his load.

Make use of him, Lance. He needs that.

Maybe Lance had found a use for Roman Charsguard.

The inside of the small house was neat to a fault. The worn couch and coffee table were at precise perpendicular angles to the walls of the room. There was a small TV and a shelf of what looked like map books, but otherwise the room was bare and very clean. The floor was dinged up old hardwood, but it looked so spotless you could do surgery on it.

"The kitchen is this way, sir," Roman said.

On the wall near the doorway to the kitchen was a large framed photo. Lance paused to look at it. The photo showed a man in camouflage kneeling on one knee, the other bent with his boot firmly on the ground. He had an arm slung over a magnificent German shepherd. The dog was glancing up at the man adoringly and the man wore a big grin.

Something hot stirred in Lance's chest.

"That's Sergeant James Patson, US Army," Roman said, his voice rough.

"His face is very pleasant."

"He was… he was the best man that ever lived." Roman swallowed hard, staring at the picture. "Strong. Kind. Honorable. Brave. He taught me what it meant to be a man."

Lance could feel the force of love that washed over Roman Charsguard as he looked at the photograph, despite the way he tried to keep the emotion off his face. Of course, a dog had to love a person that much, and be loved in return, to get the spark. But it was unusually affecting to see a tough guy like Roman so moved.

Lance wanted to ask what had happened to Sergeant James Patson, but he knew it couldn't be good. Better not to upset Roman further. And really, it was none of his business.

"This way," Roman said, his voice firming.

Lance followed him into the kitchen and accepted a cup of coffee gratefully.

"Now then, Sheriff. How can I be of service?"

"It's nothing urgent, but there's a situation I wanted you to be aware of, something you could help me be on the look-out for."

"Yes, sir."

Lance filled Roman in on the drug growers that had been setting up in neighboring counties and the violence they'd brought with them. He told him about Sam's warning. There were rumors that activity was starting up in Madera County.

Roman was immediately engaged. "We should section off the area and set up regular patrols. I'm available, sir, though we'll probably need a few more volunteers, depending on how much of the county you want to cover."

"Just right around Mad Creek."

"I'd suggest a perimeter of at least five miles, sir," Roman was standing at attention now, his eyes bright.

"Hmm. That's probably wise."

Lance narrowed his eyes at Roman. He was eager, and maybe something a little more. When Roman had opened the refrigerator to get a small carton of milk for the coffee, Lance noticed there was hardly anything in it. What did Roman do for money? He probably hunted game, living out here. How else he survived, Lance had no idea. He made a quick decision.

"I do think this is important, Roman, and I'd appreciate your help. I can't pay you full-time, but I have enough in my budget for a part-time contractor, maybe twelve-hundred a month for two months? We can see if there's a need beyond that."

An expression raced across Roman's face that was obscenely grateful. He blinked rapidly and pulled his shoulders back farther. "I'm a good choice for the job, sir. I promise you nothing unwanted will come into this territory on my watch. And… the money will be much appreciated."

His mother was right, Roman was desperate to be useful. Lance felt a stab of unease that he'd waited so long to follow up with Roman. And then he felt more unease when he realized how many others in his pack needed his help just as badly, needed jobs, needed to feel useful.

It was a good reminder why Lance was in no position to have a private life of his own.

They discussed strategy. Roman was so far ahead of what Lance had been thinking, that it quickly became clear Roman should organize the operation. He was thrilled to be put in charge of planning, and even suggested a few other quickened he could call on for patrol duty.

"Is there any particular person you suspect, sir? Any place you want me to monitor more closely?"

Lance hesitated. He didn't want to start finger-pointing at Tim Traynor, but if Roman was going to be working for Lance, he needed to be able to trust him. "There is one new guy, just moved here a few weeks ago. I'm not sure what he's up to, honestly. Have you been trained in sniffing out drugs?"

"Yes, sir."

"Do you think you'd know cannabis in plant form? Even if the plants were very young?"

"I would, sir."

"Good. I'm hoping this guy isn't doing anything illegal. But he's lied to me about a few things, and he's growing *something*. I just want to know for certain what it is."

"And you don't want him to know that you're checking up on him?"

Lance sighed in relief. "That would be ideal, yes."

"Absolutely no problem. Give me his address, and I'll do reconnaissance today."

"No, not today. His plants haven't come up yet. I'll let you know when I need you. In the meantime, you can get the rest of it organized."

"Looking forward to it, sir." Roman grinned. For a moment, he looked startlingly young and more than a little dangerous.

Lance drove back to town hoping he hadn't just tried to leash a tiger.

When Lance got into the office, he picked up another cup of coffee as he walked in the door, said hi to Leesa at the front desk, filled Charlie in on what he'd put Roman up to, and finally settled down to his email and voice mail.

His uniform felt constrictive after spending so many hours in his dog form. And the memory of the bath the night before, being shampooed and pampered by a human, made his face burn. The blush was so bright he could see it in his reflection in the window beside his desk.

Idiot.

At some point that morning, he had to talk to Bill McGurver, take his lumps in ridicule, and make sure Bill kept his mouth shut.

Christ. The things he did for this town.

The first thing that caught his eye in his email was from Sam Miller down in Fresno. It had a link to a secure website where Sam had put the background check on Tim. Lance opened it with a sense of dread. He really didn't want to find out that Tim had a record. He was surprised how badly he didn't want that.

Tim didn't have a record. In fact, there was no Timothy Traynor anywhere near Santa Barbara. Big surprise there. As for Tim Weston, he existed and his driver's license photo matched the young man currently living in the Fitzgibbons place. Age: 23. Middle name: Alan. He had no criminal record, not even a parking ticket. In fact, from the lack of data, the guy hadn't left the house since he was born.

Oh.

There was a link at the bottom to a criminal file. Tim Weston wasn't the perp, though, that was a Richard Morton Weston. The charge was domestic disturbance and child abuse. In the file were photos of a heavyset blonde woman with a bruised face and tired eyes. And a boy. Tim looked to be a frail ten or eleven. He had a black eye, split lip, and there were pictures of deep bruises on both upper arms in the shape of fingers, and a fist-sized bruise on his lower back. The neighbors had called the police. Charges were dropped and social services were assigned to follow up. That was all that was in the report.

A hot, angry stain spread across Lance's chest and shot down his arms to clench his fists on the keyboard. How could any man do that to his wife and child? He longed to find Richard Weston and show him what it felt like to be on the receiving end of a beating. The dog in him was furious. *Protect! Protect him!*

Lance shut his eyes and ground his teeth. He reminded his dog that this had happened a long time ago. There was no need to be upset about it now. But his dog had a fuzzy view of time, and seemed to be highly sensitive today. It took several rage-filled minutes for Lance to calm himself down. When the fog lifted, the leather seat of his desk chair had an ugly rip from his claws.

Holy shit.

Lance wiped his brow and took several more calming breaths. This didn't change anything. The fact that Tim had had a terrible childhood held little relevance to whether or not he was planning to grow cannabis in Mad Creek. In fact, generally speaking, criminals were more likely to come from a bad home and an abusive background.

But Lance couldn't forget Tim's face looking down at him in the rain, his eyes wet and scared, a drop of rain poised to fall from his narrow, pale chin.

Arg.

*   *   *

"Chance?"

Tim called for the dog before he was even fully awake. He yawned and stretched, and then reality settled in a little more firmly.

He had a dog.

"Chance?" he called again, grinning. He jumped out of bed and tugged on his pajama bottoms. But when he got out to the living room, there was no sign of the dog. "Chance?"

Tim searched the house, even opening up cupboard doors and looking under the bed. But Chance was nowhere to be found. How did he get out? The cabin didn't have a doggie door, and the doors and windows were all closed. Tim would have thought he'd dreamt the entire thing if not for the comforter with some black dog hair on it still on the floor, and the wet towels and wet dog smell that lingered in the bathroom.

Tim ran outside and called Chance's name, but there was no response. Chance had gone.

Tim took it hard. With dragging steps, he returned to the kitchen and made himself coffee and toast. There was a heavy weight on his chest, and he sniffed like he was getting a cold. Stupid. He should have known the dog had a home. No doubt Chance had somehow gotten out of the house and gone back to his owners. Chance was probably fine.

Tim, however, was not. He realized he must really be lonely to have bonded with Chance so fast, to have been so excited about keeping him. There was just something about Chance. He was the kind of dog Tim had always wanted—a big dog, agile but not mean. He was super-smart and cooperative. Well, sometimes cooperative. His eyes were so expressive. It almost seemed like he understood Tim. It had been a lot of fun to give him a bath and hang out. Tim had already had visions of the dog running around in the yard while he worked in the greenhouse, and keeping him company at night, someone he could talk to, someone who loved him just the way he was. Weren't dogs supposed to be like that? What did it say about

Tim that even a dog rejected him?

Well, whatever it said, Chance was gone. So much for running to the store today to pick up dog food and a collar. Tim should be glad not to have to spend the money. He didn't feel glad.

With a sigh, he got dressed and got to work.

*   *   *

Tim misted all the seed trays and checked to make sure they didn't look like they'd gotten too cold overnight. The weather report had said 55, so they should be fine. Then he set about planting more trays of Orange Glow and Mixed Popper sweet peppers.

He'd researched all the farmer's markets in the area and turned in online applications for the ones he'd found. Eventually, if he could make a go of it, he'd love to have a nursery business out here on the property. But that was way beyond his resources at the moment.

Could he really sell enough veggies and herbs to pay the rent Linda wanted, put food on the table, and keep himself stocked in seeds and supplies?

What kind of a sissy-ass skill is raising plants? Who's gonna buy shit from you when they can pick greens off the side of the road or get them carrots on sale in bulk at Costco? It was his father's voice.

Marshall chimed in. *You couldn't run a business if Donald Trump himself were sitting on your shoulder 24/7.*

Tim felt sick with a wave of dread, but he pushed the voices away. His dad wouldn't know good food if he choked to death on it, and Marshall—Marshall didn't have a crystal ball. Just because Tim had chosen to spend all his time in the greenhouse when he'd worked for Roots of Life, didn't mean he couldn't work with customers. Marshall didn't know what Tim was or wasn't capable of.

He pictured himself running a little organic produce stand in Mad Creek and people passing him by with haughty glances at his prices.

No. Don't do that to yourself.

Right. Positive thinking. He pictured himself barely able to keep up as people cooed over his produce. He'd have lovely Golden Yellow celery and big bushy Pascal Giant. There'd be tiny yellow fingerling potatoes and white Ghost carrots. He'd bought those seeds from an heirloom seed company, and they were germinating even now. Exotic and pretty—that's what the patrons at the Santa Barbara farmer's markets liked. Surely the people in Mad Creek wouldn't be all that different.

He thought with longing about his Purple Passion Pepper, with its bright grape hues and firm texture. That had always sold out at the markets. And they couldn't grow enough of his Garnet Globe carrots—which looked like red radishes and tasted like sweet carrots—to keep up with demand. If he could grow those, he'd certainly be a success.

But Tim couldn't grow any of those things. He couldn't grow them because fucking Marshall had gone behind his back and copyrighted the varieties under the Roots of Life name, leaving Tim off the paperwork. Now Tim couldn't grow them, even though he'd done every bit of the work of thinking them up and working the kinks out of the hybrids, generation after generation. It had taken him three years to get just the right color and texture for the Purple Passion Pepper and to get it to successfully repeat from seed. Roots of Life had made hundreds of thousands of dollars off Tim's hybrids. And all that time, Marshall's promises of equal share in the profits had been eaten away by *extraordinary expenses* here, *transportation damage*, and *reasonable reserves* there. And Tim had bought it hook, line, and sinker.

Ugh! He'd been such a fool! He was never trusting another person—never again.

Tim finished planting the last of the trays and checked for germination again. The top of the soil was loosening on the first tray of tomatoes he'd planted. Soon fresh green shoots would be poking up. By now it was sunny and warm and nearly noon, and there was no putting off the real work that needed to be done.

He walked out to the big scrubby area behind the greenhouse and looked at it in dismay. By the time the plants in the greenhouse were several inches tall and straining at their little allotments of soil in the tray, he had to have this field cleared and prepped for planting. It was a daunting task. At Roots of Life, Marshall would have just hired a guy to come in with a big tractor and turn it all up, then another guy to run over it and mix in the compost. But Tim didn't have those kinds of resources. What he had was his own hands and back—that's what he had.

At least Linda had some old tools in the greenhouse. There was a rusty old pick and a big shovel that wasn't the newest or the sharpest, but it was better than nothing.

93

Tim paced off the field—he needed at least 30x30 feet, and that was just to start. He marked it with stakes and twine. He spent fifteen minutes pushing the shovel into the dirt with his foot and turning over clumps and he was ready to die. God, he was out of shape! By the time it was full-on noon, and the sun was blaring, Tim was hot, sweaty, dirty, and utterly discouraged.

Of course, that was when he heard a car come down the driveway and stop. Tim leaned on the shovel, breathing hard. He slowly pulled off his work gloves. There was a fat watery bubble on the pad of his palm just below his right middle finger. Great.

He was about to go see who'd driven up when Sheriff Beaufort came walking around the corner of the house. He was carrying a large fruit basket under one arm.

Tim watched him approach with a mix of dislike, lust, and confusion. Sheriff McHotty wasn't wearing his mirrored shades today, and Tim could see the blue of his eyes when he was still quite a ways away. His black hair looked full and fluffy and his uniform was tight, as always. God, you could see the man's distinctly sculpted quad muscles as he walked, not to mention a considerable package. That ought to be illegal. Seriously.

Excuse me, officer. I want to make a citizen's arrest for indecent exposure and inciting a riot.

Tim was chuckling to himself as the sheriff walked up. The man couldn't quite meet his eyes.

"Fruit basket." Sheriff Beaufort shoved the basket toward Tim.

"I can see that. Really, that's…" Tim looked over the cellophane-covered basket. There were apples, oranges, a grapefruit, some bananas, and various bags of nuts and dried fruit. *Oh thank you, God.* This would supplement Tim's food budget nicely for a week or two. Maybe he'd been wrong about Sheriff McHotty. "Thank you," Tim said. "This is, like, the nicest thing anyone's done for me in a long time."

Blue eyes stared at him in surprise. "If that's true, that's unfortunate."

"Yeah, well…." Tim shuffled his feet. He forgot he was holding the shovel and banged his ankle into the unyielding side of it. "Ow! Fuck. Fuck!"

It hurt like a son-of-a-bitch. Tim hopped on one foot, waiting for the sharp pain to ease. The sheriff reached out a hand to steady Tim's elbow and forestall the doom of the tottering fruit basket. Tim breathed through the pain. As it slowly faded, he realized the sheriff was only a foot or so away from him and still firmly holding his arm.

95

Beaufort was a muscular but compact man, and Tim was awkwardly tall. He found himself looking down into those blue eyes. The sheriff looked right back. The man was staring again, that champion stare. Boy howdy. Only this time, it didn't feel like his stare was saying *go the fuck away*. This stare was looking down deep into Tim's soul as if trying to puzzle him out, and it was maybe even a little sympathetic. Tim felt a tingle of excitement crawl down his spine like an inch worm. It blossomed in his groin. One of Beaufort's eyebrows lifted in surprise.

Weird. Beaufort's blue eyes really were the same deep sky blue color as Chance's eyes. Or vice versa. The thought of Chance brought a wave of sorrow with it, killing the moment. Next came alarm.

Did the sheriff really drive out here to deliver a fruit basket? Or had he heard about the accident last night? Was he going to give Tim a ticket? Or worse?

"I didn't hit him on purpose!" Tim blurted out, pulling back and tripping over the shovel. *Again.* "Ow! Fuck!" Then he realized what he'd just said. To a cop. "It was a dog! Not a person or anything. The 'him' I hit. I mean, I didn't commit vehicular homicide yesterday. Or ever! Or even vehicular nudge.

Except to the dog. Who wasn't even badly hurt. You can ask Dr. McGurver. Are you here about the dog?"

Tim pinched his mouth shut, cutting off the flow of verbal diarrhea. Beaufort was probably thinking what an idiot Tim was. God, Marshall was right. He did have the social aptitude of a gnat. And for some reason, every stupid bone in Tim's body stood to attention around Sheriff Beaufort.

"I am not. Here about the dog," the sheriff said slowly and distinctly.

"Oh. Okay."

Sheriff Beaufort took a deep, calming breath, probably calling on reserves of patience to deal with *the nutso*. He looked over the field and sighed. "You're clearing a field."

"Uh... yeah."

The sheriff nodded and pursed his lips, as if he expected as much. "What are you planning to grow here?"

Tim snorted. "Well, I'm not growing drugs."

The sheriff looked at him sharply.

"I'm not! Just... you know. Vegetables. And herbs. And... stuff."

"Vegetables."

Tim barked a nervous laugh. "Heh heh. What else would I grow?"

What was the matter with him? Why was it that when he was telling the complete and factual truth—well mostly, if you forgot about the hybrid roses that didn't legally belong to him—he sounded like the biggest liar that ever lived? Why did the sheriff make him so nervous?

Sheriff Beaufort stared at him. "I don't know, Mr. *Traynor*. What else would you grow?"

Tim shrugged.

"It is Traynor, right? Timothy Traynor?"

Tim felt a blush start at his ears and flood into his face. Maybe he shouldn't have lied about that. But it was too late to take it back now. "Y-yeah."

Sheriff Beaufort rubbed his eyebrow with his thumb like he was getting a headache. "And you're going to clear this entire field. By yourself. With that shovel."

Tim looked over the vast distances of stubborn long brown grass and sighed. He didn't say anything, but a lump came into his throat. Daunting didn't begin to cover it. This was gardening by the Herculean labor method.

"Listen, Tim." Beaufort took the shovel out of Tim's hand and took it several yards away where he leaned it carefully up against a nearby tree, as if Tim might accidentally kill himself with it if it was left in his possession. Which, yeah, fair point. Then the sheriff walked back and put his hands on his narrow hips and looked into Tim's eyes.

"I don't dislike you," he said firmly.

"O—kay. That's good."

"I'm not sure what you're up to, but I don't think you're a terrible person."

Tim felt a trickle of annoyance. "Wow. I'm flattered. Can I use you as a future reference?"

"So if you're in trouble… if you think you need to do something to earn money or… or something. Something you shouldn't be. Doing. You don't, all right? You don't need to."

What? "Um, I'm not…."

"And you can come to me. Here's my card." Beaufort pulled a card out of a pocket and handed it to Tim. Yup. It had his phone number on it and everything. "If you need help. If you're running from something, or you need to talk to someone, or maybe you've gotten into something you shouldn't have, you can call me."

Tim blinked. "Thanks?"

Sheriff Beaufort looked away and straightened his back into a semblance of an ironing board. "Enjoy the fruit basket. That's all I have to say at this juncture." Without another glance, he turned and marched away.

Tim was still blinking when he heard the sheriff's car pull out and drive away.

At this juncture?

Huh. It was just possible Tim had finally met someone as bad with people as he was himself.

~6~

Playing Games

LANCE TALKED himself into going back to Tim's, and then out of it, then in—all day long.

On the one hand, he wanted to keep an 'insider status' until those seedlings came up, and until Roman had verified that they weren't cannabis. Once that was done, assuming Tim was cleared, Lance would have no reason to go back there.

On the other hand, going back felt... dangerous. Tim Weston, like most humans, didn't even know quickened existed, so it was unlikely he'd ever guess 'Chance' was more than a dog. But that wasn't what worried Lance. He was worried that it felt too comfortable to be with Tim like that. He'd always enjoyed being in dog form, even though he hadn't had much time to indulge it lately, so that was no surprise. But he was alarmed at how good it felt to be with Tim *as a dog*. He didn't want to encourage that feeling because there was no place healthy to go with that.

On the theoretical third hand, something niggled inside Lance relentlessly. The best word he had for that niggle was 'worried'. Tim appeared to be broke and friendless—digging an entire field by himself, with an old shovel. Honestly! There was just something sad about him. And that picture Lance had seen of Tim beaten-up as a child. That was the *last* thing he'd needed to see. Lance's dog instinct was already insisting Tim was pack and wanted to herd him into the fold, make sure he was safe. The photo made it ten times worse.

In the end, the dog won out. Lance didn't fight his instinct very hard. He respected and valued it too much to ignore it. So after he'd gone home for the day, he showered quickly and shifted. Then he ran the five miles through the woods to the Fitzgibbons property.

*   *   *

Tim was making himself mac and cheese when there was a scratch on the back door and a bark. He flung the door open.

"Chance! You came back!"

In an instant, the storm clouds that had been hanging over Tim all day cleared. He felt himself grinning. The dog looked up at Tim calmly, panting as if he'd been running hard. But he didn't resist when Tim sank to his knees and hugged him. He licked the side of Tim's neck and wagged his tail in a burst of doggy pleasure.

"Where'd you go? I didn't think you were coming back, so I didn't go out and buy you food."

Chance didn't look overly concerned.

"I have a can of tuna. Will that do?"

Chance brushed by Tim and sat on the kitchen floor. It was getting nippy out, and Tim closed the door on the dark with a shiver. He put down a clean bowl of water for Chance, which he drank.

"Where's your bandage, huh? Doc said you needed that." Chance ignored him. The leg didn't look swollen or anything.

Tim went back to making his mac and cheese, though he couldn't stop smiling.

"You're kind of a jerk running out on me like that," Tim scolded him lightly. "I thought you must have gone back to your owners. Maybe you're just a free spirit, huh? He Who Shall Not

Be Leashed. No ties on you, is that it, Chance?"

Chance had no comment.

"Uh-huh. You've probably got an owner in every port, am I right? A hambone here, a grooming appointment there, a cushy bed somewhere else. I've got your number." Tim chatted aimlessly, hardly even aware of what he was saying. Every so often, Chance barked in agreement.

Now that Chance was back, and larger than life sitting in Tim's kitchen, he was able to reassess the dog. Last night seemed like a dream in a way, but there Chance was in the bright kitchen light. He really was a handsome and healthy-looking dog. His fur was super thick and still silky from the bath. It was so black it had blue undertones. There was a small patch of snow white on his chest and a dot of it on one ear, like a snowflake had landed there. His eyes were that brilliant sky blue, and he watched Tim intently. Even though Chance appeared to be relaxed, sitting on his haunches on the kitchen linoleum, there was an alertness to him that said he was ready to pounce at a moment's notice.

"Do you know what's wild? You remind me a little of Sheriff Beaufort." Tim drained the cooked noodles. "He stares at me just like that, and his eyes are the same gorgeous blue. He's gotta be the hottest guy I've ever seen in real life, but I think he's a few calls short of Bingo. If you know what I mean. Besides, he's pure alpha male, and I have this love-hate thing about men like that. Nice to look at, but they make me all nervous."

Chance's bark sounded annoyed.

"I know. I shouldn't talk bad about the guy. He brought me a fruit basket after all. Honestly, give me a nice big banana and I'll follow you anywhere." Tim snorted laughter at the stupidity of his own joke. "Too bad there were no doggie biscuits in that basket, huh?"

The mac and cheese was ready, and Tim grabbed a can of Costco tuna and opened it, putting the contents in a bowl. "Mayo? Yes? No? Guess I shouldn't risk it. I'm not sure what dogs can eat."

Tim put his bowl of mac and cheese on the table and placed Chance's bowl of tuna on the floor next to his chair. Chance walked over and looked at the bowl. Tim couldn't resist stroking his silky ears. "Thank you for coming back, Chance," Tim's voice sounded a little deep. He cleared his throat. He was not going to cry over the dog's reappearance. He might be lonely, but he wasn't entirely pathetic. "Bon appetit."

Chance gave what sounded like a resigned sigh and

delicately ate the tuna.

After Tim cleaned up the dishes, he changed into his flannel pj bottoms and brought what he thought of now as 'Chance's comforter' into the living room. Chance was sitting on the couch.

"You going to hang out with me on the couch this time, buddy?" Tim turned on the TV and arranged the comforter over both of them. After a minute, Chance relaxed and leaned against Tim. Tim put his arm around the dog and that felt perfect. He was warm and soft, and he didn't think Tim was an idiot. Or if he did, he hid it really well, and that was good enough for Tim.

"What shall we watch?" He flipped channels. When he paused on ABC news, Chance put his chin on Tim's shoulder and gave him a pathetic look. On Extreme Ice Fishing, he growled.

"No? What do you like, Chance? I don't get Animal Planet."

Tim flipped to an old Vincent Price horror movie in black and white. Chance hesitated, then gave it an approving yip.

"Yeah? Okay. As long as you don't mind if I make stupid comments. My best friend in high school and I loved to do that."

Tim tossed the remote on the coffee table and snuggled down, pulling Chance closer. The dog put his front paws on Tim's lap, and Tim tucked the comforter around him. Yeah, this was nice. His own little house and Chance to share it with him. If only it could last.

*   *   *

Tim wasn't kidding about the stupid comments. Most of them revolved around the blatant subtext or cheap effects.

"Why yes, I would like to order. I'll take one of your kidneys please, with a side of garlic bread."

"The fog machine is coming! Help!"

"But I… want you, Frank. Those rotten teeth make me so hot."

Lance was rolling his eyes internally at first, but then he realized that the comments were so dumb they were actually funny, and he found them more and more hilarious as time went on. Soon he was waiting for Tim's next remark much more avidly than he was watching the movie itself. And Lance… Lance had plenty of funny ideas, but of course, Chance couldn't say them, mores the pity.

Tim was all floppy and lanky on the couch, relaxed and cuddly and cooing over Lance when he wasn't making jokes. His hands were pure magic as they stroked and scratched his fur.

Then Tim leaned in and nudged Chance's temple playfully with his nose. Chance tried to hold himself aloof, but his reserve was a sinking ship. He turned his nose into Tim's cheek and nudged back. Warmth blossomed in his chest.

Shit. His dog really, really liked Tim.

He, Lance, liked Tim. He almost didn't care that there was a possibility Tim was growing pot.

He wondered if Tim could ever be this comfortable around him when he was Lance Beaufort. And that made Lance imagine what it would be like—him, in human form, sitting there on the couch watching a movie with Tim Weston. Of course, two guys didn't cuddle up under a blanket like this or snuggle and pet or bump noses.

Unless... Unless they did.

Something hot burned in Lance's stomach, desire and panic. What an idea! But like Tim's jokes, the longer the notion sat in his brain the less stupid and more appealing it became.

If he were himself, sitting on the couch with Tim, would Tim have his arm around Lance? Or Lance around Tim? Would Tim be goofy and affectionate like this? If Lance were in his human form, Tim might look at him as he had this afternoon when he'd brought of the fruit basket, his eyes going warm, his pulse kicking up, and his pheromones sending out tantalizing signals. *Yes. Please. Now.* Tim had confirmed as much in the kitchen—he thought Sheriff Lance Beaufort was hot.

Chance whined and jumped down onto the floor, lay down and put his head in his paws.

"You too warm? Here's let's get rid of this." Tim tossed the blanket aside and patted the couch. Lance didn't move. "Is this a bid for popcorn? 'Cause I'm thinking it is. Subtle, bud. I'm on it." He got up and went into the kitchen, humming to himself.

This was wrong on so many levels it hurt Lance's brain to even think about it. Lance should not be picturing cuddling and, yes, maybe making out with Tim Weston while in dog form. Or any other form!

But what if... what if Lance came back as himself? And just... what? Ask Tim if he wanted to hang out together? Ask for... a date?

The thought was absurd. Lance was the sheriff. He didn't

109

date. The dog side of him didn't do casual like that, not the way humans did, having sex with people they hardly knew. To Lance, people were either part of his pack or they were strangers. If they were pack, they had a specific role. There was a hierarchy—his mother, close friends, colleagues, acquaintances, weaker pack members that he had to protect. There had never been a *mate*. Lance didn't have the time or room in his life for one. And if he ever changed his mind, he certainly wouldn't choose a *full-blooded human male*.

Intermarriages occurred between human and quickened. Often. But as a fourth genner, Lance had always had the not-so-subtle view that quickened were superior to full-blooded humans, and a marriage with one was somehow marrying down. That view might have been pushed a wee bit by his dear mother. As for Tim's gender, it wasn't disturbing per se. There were bonded male couples in Mad Creek, both quickened and human. When a dog bonded, it was more about the other person's spirit than their gender. Lance personally believed the quickened were more evolved that way, more attuned to what truly mattered in a person. He trusted a quickened's judgment—or a pure dog's for that matter—far more than he did a human's.

But even so, choosing to mate with a male meant not

having children, and that was a big decision to make, one that would give his mother fits. Then again, he'd told himself that he didn't plan to ever marry and have children. So what difference did it make if Tim couldn't have pups?

Wait. *Mating*? Why was he even thinking about that? He wasn't going to mate, not with Tim or with anyone else! Why had he even—

Oh, yeah. Because he'd been thinking how lovely it was to cuddle on the couch with Tim. And if he was going to cuddle with Tim, he really ought to do it as himself, not under the guise of a dog. But human cuddling… that wrote all sorts of checks Sheriff Lance Beaufort couldn't cash.

A forlorn whine emerged from his throat. Never before had Lance's dog wanted something so badly that outright clashed with the complications of human life. And never had it seemed so much easier to just be a dog. Chance could accept affection from Tim, goof around with him, they could hang out, and it didn't mean anything. Those moments were out of Lance's reach.

Tim brought in a big bowl of popcorn. He was in his socks, and Lance appreciated the sight of his long, lean legs in the flannel pjs. Instead of starting the movie again, though, he stood in the middle of the room.

"Hey, Chance. Watch this." He threw a piece of popcorn up high with one hand and caught it in his mouth. He chewed it and grinned. "Now you. Ready?" Tim threw a piece of popcorn at Lance. Lance remained, head on paws, still as a statue. The piece of popcorn bounced off his nose and onto the floor. He ignored it.

"Oh, come on! You have to at least try."

No, I really don't.

"Chance! Come on, buddy. Watch again." Tim repeated the stupid pet trick, catching a piece of popcorn in his own mouth. "Now you. Get it, Chance! Get it!"

The piece of popcorn bounced off Lance's unmoving snout. He gave a low growl.

"Oh, you think you're too dignified to catch popcorn, huh?" Tim snorted.

Lance sighed.

"Or maybe you're too old? Can't quite move quick enough? Your eyesight going? Is that it, buddy?" Tim pouted in mock sympathy.

Another growl rumbled, clearly audible, in Chance's throat.

Tim laughed. "Okay, okay. How about this? We'll make it a game. The first one of us to miss catching the popcorn has to run around the outside of the cabin three times barking the whole time—or singing as the case may be. Deal?"

Chance sat up and narrowed his eyes. He gave a sharp bark. *Now that, I would pay to see.*

"Okay. I'll go first." Tim tossed a piece of popcorn high and caught it in his mouth, but just barely.

Lance licked his lips, sitting up straighter.

"Okay, you now. Ready?" Tim paused with the piece of popcorn in his hand.

Lance watched intently. Tim threw the popcorn. Lance snatched it out of the air and swallowed it.

"Ooh, score!" Tim gave him a distant high-five. "You think you're going to win this, don't you, tuna breath?"

Lance huffed. *Duh. Bring it, muppet.*

Tim caught his second one and so did Lance. Really, Lance was at a disadvantage, because Tim had to throw the popcorn harder and aim to get it to him, whereas all he had to do for

113

himself was toss it up. But Lance was fast and he was determined to get the projectile no matter how wild Tim's throw was. And get it he did.

You cannot win, human. Surrender.

Tim missed his thirteenth piece, which bounced off his chin. Lance snatched it mid-air before it hit the floor.

"Ooh, that hurt!" Tim pretended he'd been stabbed in the chest. "Way to show me up."

Lance barked and went to the door and stared at it.

"Yeah, yeah. I can see you're looking forward to this, Torquemada. Just let me put my shoes on."

The song Tim chose for his moonlight run was *We Will Rock You.* Lance decided to jog along so he could hear the full rendition clearly. After three laps around the cabin, Tim ran out into the big clearing behind the house and continued to sing, now tossing his bangs around like a headbanger and playing an air guitar. Lance dashed back and forth around Tim like he was on speed. It was his dog's way of laughing.

His human was happy, and that made Lance's canine delirious.

No, *Tim Weston* was happy, and that made Lance Beaufort

114

feel pretty damned good too.

But it was cold, and before long Tim was rambling on about avoiding the wrath of Vincent Price's ghost by finishing his movie, and in they went. Lance decided the damage had already been done, so he jumped back up on the couch with Tim and let himself be snuggled tight.

But when Tim went to bed later that night, Lance refused to go along despite Tim's wheedling. He slept in the living room again, curled up in the corner on the comforter.

He slipped out at dawn.

~7~

Trouble with a Tail

"LANCE JAMISON Beaufort, you have lost your ever-loving mind!"

Of course it was only a matter of time before his mother sniffed it out. Lance groaned in despair. He was so unprepared for the hellacious scene he knew he was about to witness. He would have banged his head on the desk, but he was in too big a hurry to get up and shut his office door.

"Voice down, please, Mother," he told the bristling, five-foot-three dynamo. Yes, never let it be said that Lance Beaufort wasn't an optimist.

But surprisingly, Lily did switch to a stage whisper, which meant she really was embarrassed. "I can't believe what Bill McGurver just told me! You're playing *dog* with some strange human man!"

"It's not what it looks like." Lance returned to the refuge of his desk. "And thank Bill for me next time you see him, by the way."

"Oh, fuff! As if anyone could keep anything from me! Now I wanna know what's going on! Were you really hit by this man's car? What were you even doing out there? And why are you still going back?"

"I'm not—" Lance started to lie. But the look on his mother's face dared him to try it. He rethought his words. How did she know he'd been going back? No one knew that, not even Bill McGurver.

As if reading his mind, Lily huffed. "You're as predictable as the spring rains, son of mine, and as boring as drying paint. Unless there's an emergency, you're home every night by seven, you eat dinner *by yourself*, go for a run, watch exactly one hour of TV *by yourself*, and go to bed at ten o'clock. If God ever loses his watch, he only has to look at Lance Beaufort to get back on schedule."

"I am not that predictable."

"I've called you the past three nights at nine o'clock because I wanted to make sure you're coming over Saturday night for our pack dinner. I *always* reach you at nine o'clock,

Lance. So I know you weren't home. Three nights in a row! You were at *his* house, weren't you?"

It had been four nights, actually. Four nights in a row, ever since the night Tim had 'hit' Chance. There was a frantic, hand-caught-in-the-cookie-jar sense of doom that only Lance's mother could inspire in him, and apparently it was a sensation he'd never outgrow. He felt the tips of his ears grow burning hot, and he knew they were fleshy beacons of his shame.

"I've been having trouble with my phone," he tried.

Lily took two strides to the desk, leaned over it with both hands braced on the surface, and stared.

"Okay, yes! I have been over there. But it's for work. And… and it's work related!"

"Oh? Explain that to me, because I thought you were the sheriff, not in training for a role in *Lassie*."

Lance sighed. There was no way around it. He'd have to tell her everything. So he did. He explained about overhearing Tim in the diner, about all the seed trays, and the field, and the false name, and his fears about pot growers moving into town.

"So I'm just doing a little reconnaissance, that's all. It happens to be easier in dog form. Tim—Mr. Traynor to you,

Mother—gets defensive when I try to talk to him as myself. You know how it is. I can be a little… off-putting."

"You? Off-putting?" Lily said, with oceans of sarcasm. "So you're spending time in this potential drug dealer's home as a dog. To spy on him."

Lance wanted to protest, but yeah, that was pretty much it. He shrugged.

"Lance, that's a terrible idea! This man is dangerous! What if he gets abusive, huh? What if he locks you outside in a cage overnight and you can't get out and you freeze to death?"

Lance rolled his eyes. "This is California, Mother. With my fur, I couldn't freeze to death in Alaska. Anyway, you're always saying I should spend more time as a dog. You should be delighted."

"I want you to spend more time as a dog *with us*, not with a drug dealer! What if he poisons your food just for kicks? Or sells you to a dog fighting operation? Or gets you *neutered*. Have you thought of that?"

Lance hadn't, actually. A bolt of fear accompanied by a sympathetic stab of pain made him cross his legs.

"What if he hurts you? You're completely vulnerable in

119

your dog form, Lance. Your teeth are no match for a gun or knife. If he gets rough, smacks you around, what are you going to do? Change back and punch his face? Then he'll know about us, won't he!"

"Oh for God's sake! You are so off base, Mother. Tim is probably the nicest human I've ever met. I know I said he might be growing pot, but even if he is, he's not mean or capable of violence. If you saw the way he acts... he *loves* Chance! If anything, he'll kiss me to death. He said he's always wanted a dog and he's... I'm... he's..."

His mother went absolutely still. When Lily went still, that was not a good sign. "Chance?"

Lance's ears burned hotter. "That's, uh, what he named me. My dog. When I'm there. My dog form. It was something Bill said and.... What?"

Lily came around the side of the desk, invading Lance's last remnant of protective buffer. She planted her behind on his desk and leaned in, looking in his eyes like she was taking inventory of his eyelashes.

"Oh. My. Stars. You like him."

Lance made a mocking *pfft!* sound. He found himself

avoiding her eyes, though, and looking out the window. That was submissive behavior. He forced himself to meet her gaze, challengingly.

"I told you—it's a job. A few days from now, it'll be done, and that'll be that."

Lily's eyes narrowed thoughtfully.

Lance sighed. "Look, he's growing all these trays of plants in his greenhouse, and he won't tell me what they are. So once they sprout, I'll have Roman go over there and check them out. He's trained in drug sniffing. And if he gives the all-clear, that's it. 'Chance' will disappear. And if it turns out Mr. Traynor *is* into things he shouldn't be, I'll... I'll.. arrest him."

Those words were harder to say than they should be. Already, he couldn't imagine putting Tim in handcuffs and forcing him into a car like a criminal. Maybe it would be enough to just give him a good scare. A stern talking to. A ticket to leave town.

Inside, Lance's dog whined.

Lily was still watching him with those all-seeing eyes. "And how long will this sprouting business take? Do you even know?"

"Of course I know! I looked it up. Seed germination takes ten to twenty-one days, and he started that stuff at least a week ago, so it'll be any day now."

He could see Lily's brain working away. "Why can't you just go over there at night when he's asleep and peek in the greenhouse? Why do you have to be *inside* the house?"

Lance felt an uncomfortable burn in his chest, his temper sparking. He didn't like his methods being questioned. "Initially, I wanted to check out the house too. At this point, making sure he's comfortable with Chance means I have free access to the property, inside and out, when I need it."

"Lance, son, you are playing with fire."

"I have it under control. It's fine."

Lily *tsked*. "Promise me you won't go back there."

Lance stood up and met Lily glare for glare. "I'll do exactly what I decide is necessary, Mother."

Lance had learned young that you either stood up to Lily or you got run over by her. And he wasn't the type to appreciate being run over. In fact, most of the time he said *no* to her on principle, like exercising a muscle.

Lily glared a while longer. "Fine," she said at last. "Don't listen to your older and far wiser mother. But you'll be sorry."

Lance rolled his eyes. "I'm already sorrier than you could possibly imagine. Now *you* promise *me* you won't interfere, or mention it to anyone, or poke your nose in, or follow Mr. Traynor along the street when he comes into town, or do anything else that comes into your focused little brain. This isn't your problem, it's my problem, and I've got this, and I don't want you anywhere near it. My. Territory. Understood?"

Lily snorted. "As if I would tell anyone! You think I want it spread around that my son's into puppy play?"

Lance felt his temper supernova. Yes, that was really quite an interesting sensation, the way the cells inside his chest spontaneously burst into flame. "I AM NOT INTO PUPPY PLAY! AND HOW DO YOU EVEN KNOW THAT TERM?"

Lily waved her hand as if he was being silly. "Please. Like I was born fifty years old."

"I want to be stricken dead. Right now," Lance groaned and hid his face.

"Oh, all right. Fine! You're doing some reconnaissance in your dog form, and that's all it is, and it's none of my business, and I've always been a virgin. You and your brothers and sister were all conceived by supernatural means. Happy?"

Lance was exhaling and inhaling through his nose like a bull.

"Oh relax! You're going to give yourself a heart attack. I'll see you later, huh? And don't forget dinner on Saturday. Seven sharp. *Chance*."

With that Lily walked out, all but switching her invisible tail.

*   *   *

Lily knew there was more to this 'work' than Lance was saying. She could feel it. Something was different about his dog spirit. It felt more surfaced, open… happy. Besides, when Lance got all stubborn and refused to budge—

Well, to be fair, he was always like that.

But still, there *was* something going on with this ridiculous charade. Lily was not fooled. But naturally, Lance would never admit it or stop doing whatever he was doing.

There was nothing for it. She had to go see this mysterious Timothy Traynor for herself. She called Leesa at the sheriff's office.

"Leesa! I need you to do me a favor. Call me and let me know when Lance goes out on a call that'll take a while. But don't let him know I asked you or that you told me."

There was no point prevaricating. Everyone in town knew that Lily had to know everyone's business, and Leesa, as her son's receptionist, knew it so well it was probably etched on her immortal soul.

"Will do, Lily," said Leesa in a bored voice.

"Thank you!"

Now she just needed an excuse. Maybe a fruit basket?

*   *   *

Tim hated this fucking shovel. No matter how much he wrapped up his hands, it still hurt like hell to operate the damn thing, thanks to all his broken blisters. Fortunately, after the first thirty minutes or so of agony, his hands got so numb the pain faded. Then he only had to deal with the sore muscles in his thigh from stepping down on the shovel edge to sink it in the dirt, and the ache in his back from prying up each orangey-brown clod.

Frustrated, he looked over the bit he'd finished. He'd gotten less than a quarter of the area he needed turned in three long, painful days. His seedlings would be coming up any time now, and the last frost date was the tenth of May. They'd need to be transplanted to the field in just a few weeks. Then there were the peas and lettuces that need to be started in situ right away. He'd called around about hiring a guy with a backhoe, but couldn't justify spending several hundred dollars on it when his bank account was a one-way street, and those same hundreds could be spent on more seeds. Or fertilizer. Or mac and cheese. So, on he went.

He left off to do a midday check on his seedlings in the greenhouse, and that's where he found the stranger. She was looking over his seed trays. What the hell?

"Um... hello?" Tim said warily.

She was a small woman—maybe five-foot-three and slender. She didn't seem at all embarrassed to have been caught snooping. "Hi. Timothy Traynor? I'm Mrs. Beaufort, but you can call me Lily. I came to drop off a coffee cake. That's why I stopped by." She waved in the direction of a baking pan covered by a dishcloth that was sitting on the counter.

"Oh. Um. That was nice of you. Wait—" *Beaufort.* Tim looked over the black hair and sky blue eyes and felt himself unaccountably blush. "Are you related to Sheriff Beaufort?"

"I'm his mother." She sounded proud of that fact and very certain. Well, duh. She *would* be certain, wouldn't she?

"You don't look old enough to be his mother."

Tim hadn't said it as a compliment, but he could tell from the way she relaxed a little that she took it as one. "Oh. Thank you. Lance, my son, he's the sheriff."

"I… know that?" Tim said.

"He's a good man."

Tim nodded politely. If she said so.

"He's too serious, but he does have a lot of responsibility on his shoulders. Watching out for trouble. Because trouble—we don't want that here."

Tim blinked into her blue eyes. She was talking to him very pointedly. "Okay."

"So maybe you should grow your… *plants…*" she waved her hand around the greenhouse. "Somewhere else. Fresno's

127

warmer."

"Excuse me?"

Tim took a step backward toward the door. Lily Beaufort was migrating toward him, edging into his space in a way that pushed him to retreat.

"Plus, more people to buy… whatever it is you're selling. Lots more. In Fresno. Or Oakhurst even. That's far enough away. What about Mariposa?"

Tim hadn't realized he was still moving until he felt the knob of the greenhouse door press into his back. She was regarding him with a cocked head and an intent, challenging look that made her seem much larger than she actually was. Something inside him wanted to turn around and flee.

Instead, Tim got pissed. He was tired of being bullied! And what was it with this town, anyway? People were either so friendly you could hardly believe it, like Daisy at the diner, or that hyper-enthusiastic guy at the post office, Mr. Beagle, who talked Tim's ear off anytime he got within three feet of the place. Seriously, you passed by the post office door at your own peril. Or the townspeople were *Beauforts,* which… yeah. Someone needed to teach that family about a little word called 'boundaries'.

Tim put his hand behind his back to grasp the knob, stepped to one side, and pulled the door open. "Thanks for the coffee cake. But if anyone needs to leave here, Mrs. Beaufort, it's you. Nice to meet you. Bye."

Lily startled, like she was shocked he'd say such a thing to her. But she was the one who'd been rude first! He wasn't going to apologize.

She continued to stare at him, but she took a step back. "Why did you choose Mad Creek, Tim?"

"Because! Because I know Linda Fitzgibbons, the woman who owns this property, and we made a deal. I'm allowed to live here rent-free in exchange for a plant hybrid I'm growing for her. And that's, you know, a key selling point because I don't have the money! I lost my job, and I'm trying to get back on my feet, so, my apologies, but I'm not going to be run off! Not by you or your son or anyone else!"

Lily hrmphed, but her intensity deflated. She turned to look over the plants with a casual air like they hadn't just argued, the two of them, complete strangers. She wandered to a tray and poked at the dirt.

"Could you please not—"

"The plant hybrid for Linda Fitzgibbons… what does that mean?"

Her tone was nicer now. Curious. But Tim didn't trust her past the end of her nose. "It's a rose," he said sullenly. He regretted it once he'd said it. But Lily Beaufort didn't know anything about Roots of Life or Marshall, or where Tim had gotten the rose hips. There was no reason not to tell the truth.

"We have yellow roses in our yard," Lily said. "They must be strong, because we never do a thing to them. They're pretty but they get spots."

"That's probably blackspot. Or possibly fungus. Do they get full sun?"

Lily shrugged. "They're against the front of the house, which faces east."

"If they're against the house, they get shade at least half the day from the house's shadow. If they get four hours of sun a day, they should be all right, but there's some organic spray you can get for blackspot. It's worth it. Also, be sure to clean up any fallen leaves regularly, because the disease harbors in the leaves."

Lily looked at him assessingly, but she continued to stroll

away, looking around. "So these roses you're growing are yellow roses? Red?"

"With a hybrid, you breed two different rose species, so you don't know exactly what you'll get until the hybrid plant blooms. But yes, I have some nice crosses that should be yellow. The one I hope to get for Mrs. Fitzgibbons, though, is a cream with lavender tips."

"Sounds nice." She didn't look very impressed.

"It *will* be, if I succeed. It's really hard to get. Plants with tips are almost always red or pink. No one's ever done a tipped lavender. Not the shade I'm going for anyway. If I pull it off—" Tim shut his mouth. No point getting into that. Mrs. Beaufort would probably think he was just some loser wannabe, and he wasn't about to recount his awards and stuff. Anyway, why was he telling her anything?

Lily turned and gave him a smile. "You know, plants have always fascinated me."

"They have?"

"Oh, yes! Green things! Growing! Life!" Her nose did a weird little quiver. "I'd love to hear more about all this. What do you say we go in and have some coffee and coffee cake? I can

131

see you've been working like a slave, Tim. You deserve a break."

"Well, I—"

Lily grabbed the coffee cake, linked her arm in his, and led the way.

Over coffee and coffee cake, Tim told Lily about Roots of Life.

He told her about Purple Passion Pepper and the awards.

He told her about Marshall, the bastard, and the profits he'd kept for himself and the copyrights he'd filed and how that meant Tim couldn't grow his own hybrids.

Tim had seen a documentary once about how certain carnivorous plants lure in food with tiny, fine, hair-like cilia, which wave and wave and gradually draw the speck of food—or fly as the case might be—down into their gullet. Talking to Lily Beaufort was like that. Her eyes were like information vacuums and her sympathetic little murmurs were like the tiny waving cilia hairs drawing out his life story with seductive ease.

And maybe Tim had been in need of someone to talk to, because he could *not* shut up.

They drank a pot of coffee and ate the *entire* coffee cake. Lily had quite an appetite for being such a petite little thing.

"You're going to be a huge success," Lily said matter-of-factly, as she cleaned the last crumbs off her plate. "I'll tell all my friends to go see you at the Mad Creek farmer's market."

"Thanks. I'd appreciate that," Tim said sincerely.

"But you really shouldn't be doing all this on your own!" she said with a motherly *tsk*. "It's way too much work. And you shouldn't spend so much time by yourself out here. It's not healthy for a boy your age. People might get the wrong idea. Particularly stupid people."

"I'm not alone. I have Chance." Tim felt a sudden wave of affection and wished the dog was there right now.

"Chance?" Lily asked with wide-eyed curiosity.

"He's my dog. At least, I hope he is."

"Well, where is he?" Lily looked around.

"He, um, well, I'm not sure where he goes during the day, but he's only around at night. I think maybe he has another home. Hey, maybe you know him? He's some type of collie, I think, really thick black hair, brilliant blue eyes. He has a white spot here—" Tim placed a hand over his heart. "And a tiny spot

133

here—" he touched his ear, smiling at the thought of it. "Honestly, he's the most beautiful dog you ever saw."

"Doesn't sound at all familiar," Lily said dryly.

"Well, Dr. McGurver said Chance didn't belong to anyone in the area, and he would know, right? Maybe Chance just likes to wander during the day. Whatever, he's awesome company. We're fine, just the two of us."

Lily hummed. "Sounds like he's an older dog. Probably boring. Set in his ways."

"He's not boring, but he is stubborn," Tim grinned. "Sometimes I think he gets *me* to do what *he* wants."

"I know the feeling." She looked at him with those overly bright eyes. "He's sedentary, though, I'll bet. Of course, you work hard all day so you don't need an active dog. Maybe a couch potato lump is what you need."

Tim laughed. "You don't know Chance. Last night we took a long hike through the woods and he showed me a new trail. Of course, he does like to watch movies with me too. But we take dance breaks." He smiled at the memory of the two of them jumping around while watching *Austin Powers* last night.

Lily choked on her coffee. "D-dance breaks?"

134

Tim felt stupid now. Why had he said that? "Just, you know, being silly. It's easier to be yourself with an animal."

Lily huffed.

"I never had a dog before but… yeah. Chance is brilliant. Maybe I need a break from people right now." His chest grew hot and tight, and he fell silent, sipping his coffee.

You're a fucking loser, and you'll always be a fucking loser.

Maybe he needed a break from people for a long time, actually.

Lily patted his hand. "Nonsense. What you need is a nice girl. One with two legs."

Tim snorted at the odd remark and hesitated. But he wasn't going to be afraid, not about this. And Lily had already dragged everything else out of him. If she decided she didn't want to tell her friends about his produce stand, so be it.

"I'm gay," he said firmly. "So no, no girls, two-legged or otherwise."

Lily tilted her head and regarded him thoughtfully but didn't seem particularly offended. All she said was, "Well."

135

They drank the rest of their coffee in silence.

~8~

Seeds of Despair

ROMAN DIDN'T like the looks of that black truck. He'd seen it twice before on his patrols. The first time he'd seen it cruising through town with its tinted windows in the back and its shiny, low-riding chassis barely inches off the road. Through the front windows, he could see two men—driver and passenger, both dark-haired and swarthy, both wearing sunglasses.

He hadn't thought too much of it the first time he'd seen them. The second time they'd driven past him, slow, while he was patrolling the hilly northern neighborhood along Broad Eagle Drive. He'd looked at the driver as the truck passed, but the driver and passenger did not look back.

Humans look back when someone stares at them. Unless they are very deliberately trying not to.

Now the truck was parked at the turn-out at the top of Broad Eagle Drive. There was a viewpoint overlooking the downtown part of Mad Creek. One of the men was leaning against the hood of the truck watching the road. The other was standing at edge of the overlook. That man was trying to look casual, arms crossed, but Roman could see there was something he was holding in his right hand, half-hidden by his body.

It was a pair of black binoculars.

Roman rolled into the pull-out and turned off his truck. He waited a moment before getting out. He had a wave of insecurity. He wished Sergeant James Patson were there. James would know what to do. Roman had always relied upon his judgment. But James wasn't there, and Roman had a town to protect. He'd been asked to help by Sheriff Beaufort, and he wanted to help, more than anything.

He checked that his firearm was safely snapped into its holster at his back, put on his jacket, and stepped out of his car.

"Nice day." The man who was leaning against the truck spoke casually as Roman approached. He had a faint Hispanic accent.

It was true enough, but then it was April, and the days were warming up even if nights were still a little cold. It was almost always nice.

138

Roman stopped a few feet from the stranger. The hair on the back of his neck bristled and he wanted, badly, to bark and bare his teeth. There was something about these strangers he didn't like, something threatening. He swallowed the urge.

"Where are you from?"

"L.A. We're on vacation, eh, Bro?" The man at the truck looked at the other man, who grunted in confirmation. Roman couldn't see their eyes behind their sunglasses. He wasn't sure if they were lying. Sometimes he could hear it in the change of a human's heartbeat or smell it in a fresh wave of sweat, but only if the person cared that they were lying.

"Where are you staying?" Roman asked, his voice rough.

The man leaning against the car exchanged a look with his friend. "Man, chill. We're not doin' nothin' wrong. Just enjoyin' the view."

"I didn't say you were."

"And you're not even a cop."

It felt like a slap in the face. *You have no authority*. But Roman *was* on the sheriff's department's payroll, even if only briefly. "Just making conversation."

The two men said nothing.

139

Again, Roman felt a surge of self-doubt. If he and James were facing this situation, Roman would be pulling at the leash and making it clear to the men that they weren't welcome, while James would be holding him back. James would play it tough but cool, letting the threat of Roman stand without forcing the issue. But now Roman had to be himself *and* James. He had to hold himself back and obey the law. It left him on uncertain ground.

"Have a nice stay," Roman said at last. "I'm sure I'll see you around." *I'll be watching you.*

He got back into his car and turned it around, headed slowly back down the hill.

He would put it in his report. Sheriff Beaufort would tell him what they should do.

*   *   *

Lance had stopped even trying to fight his dog. Chance wanted to be with Tim—wanted it full-on with all his dog's instinctual joy, focus, and anxious sense of duty. So. Lance let him.

He told himself all of this was short-lived anyway, so he

might as well let his dog enjoy it while he could. Nothing like this would ever happen again. And it was interesting to learn more about his dog nature, like how open its heart was, and how much pleasure it got in loving and being loved without any sexual component to it, any awkwardness, or any need to do or say the right thing. His dog was so much better at that than Lance was.

Once this was over, he had to make more of an effort to get out, be with others, maybe find someone he could at least date. Maybe he could even be friends with Tim. His dog was inspiring him.

Every night for a week, Chance slept on the floor of Tim's living room after spending the evening hanging out. Every morning before Tim awoke, he shifted back into Lance, checked the greenhouse to see if the trays had sprouted yet—no, they hadn't—shifted back and ran home to get ready for work.

Honestly. He was beginning to think Tim didn't know what the fuck he was doing with those plants.

"I don't know what's up with my seedlings," Tim muttered as he stood at the counter making chicken roll-ups for supper. "They should have been up days ago. I mean, one or two bad seeds, yeah, but *all* of them? I thought maybe it's been too cold in the greenhouse at night, even though the temperature gauge says it's not. I bought a space heater today and got it up and running. Made some nice compost tea. I don't know what else to do. This has never happened to me before."

Tim talked to Chance all the time, about everything. That night he was really upset. Lance could hear it in the abrasive edge to his voice, feel it in Tim's dull, angry heartbeat, and see it in the ugly tension near his mouth. He wished he could reassure Tim. On the other hand, it was a relief not to be able to talk, because as sure as the sun rose, Lance Beaufort would fuck it up.

He waited until Tim put his dog bowl with two chicken roll-ups on the floor and then licked Tim's hand. Tim took the hint and put his own plate on the table, then squatted down and hugged Chance tight.

"You're just trying to butter me up so I forget there're a dozen cans of dog food I bought in the cupboard that you refuse to eat. Princess Picky Pot."

Chance huffed. He put one paw on Tim's knee, the closest he could get to returning the hug.

"Well, enjoy the food while it lasts, bud, because if I can't even grow *vegetables* anymore, I'm hosed." He sighed. "We'll both be dumpster-diving this fall."

Chance's ears perked up at the word 'vegetables'. Tim got up and slumped into his chair, still depressed. He poked at his food.

There was no reason for Tim to lie to Chance. Then again, that didn't mean he was *only* growing vegetables. Still, Lance was becoming more and more certain this entire exercise had been for naught. He felt stupid. But there were a whole lot of undefined emotions underneath that, a myriad of doggie and human emotions that fit under the general umbrella of 'worry' and 'longing'.

Tim's phone buzzed. The few times that had happened, Chance had seen Tim look at the display and refuse the call. But tonight, he was so out of it he answered the phone without thinking.

"Hello?" Tim tensed up immediately. "What do you want, Marshall?" Tim got up and restlessly began to pace. "Who told you where I am?"

Lance whined. Anger and fear and hurt wafted off Tim in waves.

"That's none of your business! Well, go ahead and call the police. I didn't take any of your—*my*—damn seeds. I quit, remember! You don't own me anymore!"

143

Tim hung up the phone and nearly threw it across the room before he seemed to remember he didn't want to break it. Instead, he held down the power switch until it went to sleep, then he tossed it on the kitchen table.

"I hate that guy!" Tim shouted at Chance. Then he deflated and went back to his chair. He sat there poking at his roll-ups.

Lance wanted to ask, *Who's Marshall?* He wanted to ask, *You said he knows where you live. Are you in danger?* He wanted to say, *You're in trouble. Why? How can I help?* But Chance was only a dog, not a friend or a partner, so he couldn't say anything.

For the first time, Lance wished he was in Tim's life as himself. But Lance Beaufort hadn't earned that right and, honestly, didn't deserve it.

Lance did his best to cheer Tim up that night. Tim went out to the dark greenhouse to check the seed trays again after supper and Chance padded along. Tim poked at the soil a little, his face unhappy, but nothing had sprouted.

They watched a romantic comedy on TV. Tim, still unusually quiet, lay down on the sofa and patted the space next to him. Chance lay down beside Tim, and Tim covered them both with the comforter.

Chance was turned away from Tim, but he felt the shudders in his human's body. Tim was crying.

No. Enough was enough!

Chance jumped off the couch and barked sharply until Tim sat up. "What is it?"

Chance ran around back and forth across the room, his tongue lolling.

"I know, I'm terrible company tonight," Tim sighed.

Chance barked and spun around chasing his tail until Tim laughed.

"Geez, you're a goof. Okay, okay! What do you want to do?"

Chance ran to the door and barked eagerly, wagging his tail. *Come on, Tim. Liven up.*

"Moonlight walk?"

Chance barked.

Tim huffed as if he was too tired to move. But Chance didn't let up until Tim went to the coatrack and put on his beat-up Converse tennies and coat.

"Maybe I do need the fresh air. Race you?"

They walked for an hour, Chance running ahead and back and nudging gently into Tim's side so as not to trip him. Tim ghosted a hand over Chance's head when he was close and managed to keep up with the playful pace. By the time they got back, Tim was in a much better mood. That night, before he went to bed, Tim put Chance's comforter on the living room floor and then sat down cross-legged on it himself. Chance lay down, and Tim stroked his ears for a while.

"Thank you for being here with me. I love you, Chance. If I didn't have you...." His voice wobbled, and he didn't finish the sentence.

Shit.

A few minutes later, Tim kissed Lance on the head and went to bed.

Lance couldn't sleep. *I love you, Chance.* God. But then, he'd already felt that, hadn't he? The strength of Tim's love was like a blanket of light—pure and good and basic. It called to

146

Lance's dog in a way that, not only was hard to resist, it felt *wrong* to resist it. And even though Lance rationally told himself that Tim only loved a dog, not him, not *really*, it still felt like a precious gift. How was Tim going to feel when Chance vanished? He would be without any support at all.

Lance hated that. The poor guy was struggling enough. Why? Where were Tim's family and friends? Who was Marshall? And why weren't Tim's plants coming up? He *seemed* to know what he was doing. At this point, Lance would be happy to see Tim succeed at anything, even if it was growing cannabis. Hell, he'd roll a doobie in celebration.

Christ, he'd gotten way too attached. Maybe his mother had been... not entirely off base? Right-ish? It galled him to admit it.

He heard a muffled cry. Lance tensed, his head rising and his ears tilting toward the bedroom. "No! Stop it!" Then, "Dad, no!"

Lance jumped to his feet and ran into the bedroom.

Tim was having a nightmare. He was tangled in his sheets and sweating, even though the house was cool. His face was relaxed and strained at the same time. "Not my fault!" He jerked in his sleep, like he'd been hit. He whimpered in pain.

Lance didn't think about it. He jumped onto the bed and lay down next to Tim and nudged Tim's face with his nose. He whined.

He felt it when Tim woke up, the dark pull of the nightmare evaporating. He could hear the pounding of Tim's heart, smell his fear. Tim threw an arm around Chance, pulled him closer, turned his face into his pillow, gave a quivering sigh, and went back to sleep.

Lance stayed.

~9~

Party Hounds

LANCE PARKED in his mother's driveway on Saturday night, dreading the evening. He'd much rather be hanging out at Tim's. But Lance was already skating on thin ice with Lily. He had to show her he was perfectly capable of not going over to Tim's house, that he was not spending too much time over there as a dog.

Even though he was totally spending too much time over there as a dog.

He grabbed the case of Samuel Adams from the passenger seat and got out of the cruiser.

Inside, the pack gathering was as rambunctious as usual. His brothers Lonnie and Ronnie were there with their wives and broods. Fred Beagle, from the post office, was chatting in his usual animated fashion with Daisy, from the diner. The newly quickened members of the pack were in attendance, including

149

Gus, the bulldog. He appeared much less lost than he had when Lance had met him for breakfast. His eyes were bright with happiness, and he eagerly stood close to Bill McGurver, drinking in everything the man said.

Lance envied Gus his simple enjoyment of company. Maybe somewhere along his genetic pool, he'd become too human. Usually, he liked these gatherings. Even though he never said much, he liked having all the pack in one place where he could see them, assess their wellbeing, know they were safe and in good spirits. It was... less fragmenting when they were all in one spot. But that night far too much of Lance's nature was focused on Tim and wanted to be *there*. It just wasn't the same.

Bill McGurver noticed Lance, gave him a nod and a smile from across the room and then, as if remembering, looked guilty.

Yeah, Bill, we'll have a little talk about your epic betrayal to my mother later.

Lance greeted his nieces and nephews, kissed his sisters-in-law on the cheek, traded jibes with his brothers, and at long last, as if running a gauntlet, got the case of beer into the kitchen. His mother was there stirring a huge pot of spiced peanut butter cider and chatting with a voluptuous dark-haired woman. The woman was Lance's age, and she wore a tight gold sweater. She managed to display her assets while coming off as classy. She was just the type his mother would— *Uh-oh.*

"Lance!" His mother came over and gave him a one-armed hug. She relieved him of the beer. "You remember Janine Donegal? She recently moved back to Mad Creek."

Lance did recognize her now, more by her smell than anything. The Donegal family had been in Mad Creek for a good twenty years. Janine's parents were both second gens that had met in Mad Creek. That was the sort of bloodline his mother praised. The last Lance had heard, Janine had taken a high-flying lawyer job in San Francisco after college. He had nothing against Janine, she was pretty and no doubt intelligent, but he didn't like mother's yenta-ish scheme. Lily was being so obvious she might as well be skywriting it. *Lance + Janine 4ever.*

"Welcome back." Lance held out his hand, and Janine shook it, sliding her hand along his first in a typical quickened rub. Her grip was firm, and her smile was genuine.

"Hi, Lance! I remember you. Always the quiet one of the Beaufort brothers! So you're the sheriff now? Your mom was just telling me about it."

I'll bet she told you my underwear size too, the side of the bed I lie on, and about the pulled muscle in the groin I got last year.

"Yup. It's not terribly exciting in a place like Mad Creek, and I like to keep it that way. What brings you back?"

Janine shot Lily a knowing look. "Does anyone ever leave Mad Creek for long? It gets wearying not being able to be yourself out there. I'd been hoping to move back for the past few years, but my firm got bought out last month and it was a great opportunity to grab a decent severance package. I'll be setting up a small legal practice here." She gave Lance a cheeky grin. "Maybe I can represent all those criminals you rake in."

Lance snorted. "I'll do my best to stir up some traffic for you."

Janine's mother stuck her head in the kitchen doorway. "Janine? Are you busy? There's someone I want you to meet."

"Nice seeing you again, Lance," Janine said before slipping away. Her pleasant grace and straight-forward cheerfulness *was* appealing. If Lance remembered correctly, her people were descended from Labradors. She could be a big help to Mad Creek, especially if she was willing to take on pro bono work. The people who needed the help most here didn't have money.

"I see you approve," Lily said, with a dog-that-ate-the-bone smile. She pulled a tray of meatballs out of the oven. "Hold that bowl for me, would you?"

Lance held the bowl while his mother discharged the meatballs into it. "You're real subtle, Mom. I can see the grandpups dancing in your eyes."

Lily gave a nasty little chuckle that Lance didn't care for at all. "Oh, aren't you the center of the universe? As it so happens, I intend nothing of the kind. My role is simply to bring the single young people of our community under one roof and provide food and hospitality. How they pair off is their own affair. I happen to think you'll have to work for Janine if you want her. She's quite a catch."

He grunted and set the bowl of meatballs on the table. "See, that right there is how you *should* feel. But the day you let things take their natural course without interfering is the day I shift into a walrus."

"You have put on a few pounds. And you're getting a bit long in the tooth."

"I have not put on a few pounds!"

"Evening." Roman Charsguard wandered into the kitchen holding two bottles of wine. He was red in the face and smelled

153

of uneasiness. "Didn't know if I should bring red or white, so...."

His mother took the bottles with a big smile. "I'm so pleased you joined us, Roman!"

"Well. You sort of blackmailed me."

"Oh, fuff! I would have given your mail back eventually. It's on the hutch in the dining room. But don't grab it and run! You might as well eat while you're here. We have plenty of food."

"Lance," Roman nodded at him.

"Hey, Roman."

Roman was ill at ease in the house, or maybe it was the crowd. But Lance was happy to see him out for a change. He had to admit, his mother did work wonders in their community. That was Lily. She was the best of times and the worst of times all rolled into one tight little border collie package.

Lance clasped Roman's shoulder, giving him what he hoped was a grounding pat and turned them both toward the living room. "Hey. I got the report on that black truck you saw. It's legally registered in Los Angeles, and it's not missing or stolen. But I thought—"

Lance's words, and the thoughts behind them, evaporated, never to be heard from again.

Across the room was Janine. Janine was talking to *Tim Weston.*

Tim.

Weston.

It was strange and disturbing seeing him someplace other than his house, his house where he was just Chance's human. Here Tim was a young man at a party talking to a beautiful woman, familiar and new at the same time. He looked really good. He had on a dark green button-down shirt that brought out the gold tones in his sandy brown hair and his hazel eyes. It was tucked into fitted jeans that showed off his long legs and slim hips. He looked tall and shy. And from the way Janine was looking at Tim, he was very attractive.

Of course he's attractive. He's attractive to you, *isn't he?*

"Lance, is something wrong?" Roman growled, reading Lance's tension and going instantly on guard.

Lance hurried to reassure him. "No! No, it's nothing like that. Honestly. I just... excuse me for a minute. I need to talk to my mother."

Lance dragged Lily out the back door where they'd be less likely to be overheard. As usual, she didn't take him seriously.

"Oh, relax! Don't have a conniption fit. I met Tim while I was out shopping, and he seemed like a nice boy and so very lonely. So I invited him to the party. Half the town's here anyway. It's no big deal."

"But it's a pack party!"

Lily waved a dismissive hand. "We have humans in the pack." They did, but the few they had were spouses of quickened or those, like old Doc Benton, who knew about the pack by necessity and could be trusted not to tell outsiders. "Besides, I told everyone there would be a human who isn't in the know here tonight. No one's going to howl at the moon. Well, not literally anyway."

Everything Lily said made some sort of sense by itself, but the whole thing wasn't computing. Lily had clearly run around Lance, but he wasn't sure how far she'd run around him or what the full implications were. What was she up to?

"But... but what if Tim *is* growing you-know-what! I'm still investigating him!"

156

Lily snorted. "Any fool can see that boy is not a drug lord. And if he does grow a little pot, well, big deal. I used to enjoy reefer now and then. It makes you nice and loose for sex."

"Mother!"

She rolled her eyes. "I swear, we should never have let you play fetch when you were an adolescent. Obviously one of those sticks got lodged up your behind. Now I have to go back in and stir that cheese sauce or it'll burn. Try to socialize, Lance. You might actually enjoy it."

Lance followed his mother back inside, huffed his way past her in the kitchen to show his displeasure, and stalked into the living room. He found himself marching right up to where Tim was being chatted up by Janine Donegal.

The presumptuous bitch.

"Oh. H-hi, Sheriff." Tim recognized him without his uniform. That was a good sign. But he also looked skittish and unhappy to see him.

Lance's stomach sank. *Oh yeah right.* He himself had moved ahead in his feelings about Tim. But Tim was still standing still at that 'bat-shit crazy sheriff guy' first impression (okay third impression—at least he'd done the fruit basket). And

Lance realized that this right here—this party—was an opportunity. It was a chance to talk to Tim *as himself* and maybe push past that point. And suddenly that seemed like the most important thing in the world.

Lance crowded into his rival's space a little more, nudging Janine out of the way.

"Hmm. Right." She sounded confused. "Excuse me. I'll, uh, go see if Lily needs help."

Lance was staring at Tim's face and ignored Janine, though he was puffed up in a possessive warning. Tim had his eyes slightly downcast, which more or less translated to Lance's chest. His face was a little pink. Neither of them responded.

"Okay then!" Janine left Lance's peripheral vision. The air lightened perceptibly. Lance's heart was pounding.

Say something nice. Come on.

"I, um, take it you've met my mother. Lily? Lily Beaufort?"

A smirk turned up Tim's lips, and he lifted his eyes. "Yeah. She's something else."

"Truer words. Can I get you something to drink?"

Tim looked down at the Coke can in his hand. "I have something."

"Something else? Beer? I brought Sam Adams. And there's Dos Equis in the fridge. Or wine. Red or white. I don't know what kind, though. Or if it's any good. I think the bottles have a cork. Some people care about that."

Tim gave him a tentative smile. "Thanks, but I probably shouldn't drink. I have to drive home. Wouldn't want the sheriff getting on my case." He tittered nervously.

"I can drive you," Lance said firmly.

"Um... but then my car would be here?"

"I can pick you up tomorrow and bring you back here to get your car."

Tim just blinked at him.

Okay. Too much. Back off, big boy. It was hard. His dog was incredibly excited to see Tim, as if he hadn't seen him in *ages*! He was jumping around inside making Lance feel crazy. Add in the natural possessiveness that had swamped him seeing Tim talk to Janine, and Lance wanted to pounce on Tim and drag him home. Or... or something.

He wanted Tim to like him—for him. Or at least not

despise him. That would be a start.

Lance swallowed. "Or... you can drink Coke. Whatever you want. It's your choice."

Tim arched an eyebrow. "It is, huh? Thanks."

Lance sighed. "So. How are you settling in to Mad Creek?"

Tim shrugged, but his mouth tugged downward. "I've been working hard, but I'm not seeing a lot of progress, to be honest."

Lance could feel the waves of unhappiness coming off Tim. It seemed his dog was still in tune with Tim's moods, even when he was in human form.

"Sorry to hear that."

"Well, ya know." Tim held up his can with a wry smile. "I figured a chance to party hard was a nice break."

"I meant it earlier. If you want to drink tonight, I'd be happy to take you home, and make sure you get back to your car tomorrow. I do patrols around town all the time, so it's not any extra driving for me."

Lance's voice had softened now that Janine was gone, sounding less demanding, and Tim seemed to soften with it.

"Really?" He bit his bottom lip and regarded Lance as if he

was trying to make a decision.

Lance made a cross on his chest. "Dog's honor."

Tim frowned a little in confusion but laughed. "Okay. Yeah. I wouldn't mind drinking."

"What can I get you? Beer or wine? Or if you like mixed drinks, I can make you a rum and Coke."

"I'll take a Sam Adams."

Lance felt a smile spread across his face. He felt stupidly happy that Tim had chosen the drink he'd brought to the party, as if that meant anything. "I'll go get it."

*　　　　　*　　　　　*

By the second beer, Tim was in a much better mood. It'd been a good decision to come out tonight. He wasn't exactly a social butterfly, and he hardly knew anyone in town. But Lily had been convincing. And he needed a change of scenery, a break from the depressing, incomprehensible failure that was his greenhouse.

Having the hottest guy in town talking to him made Tim feel like he'd won a temporary visa to leave his pathetic life for a single night, like Cinderella. It was nice not feeling like a wallflower. And more than that, it felt… good. Being physically close to Lance. Which was weird. Apparently, Tim's hormones were way ahead of his brain. Maybe because they were at a crowded party, Tim could allow himself to be attracted to the alpha male without fear of what he might do if they were alone.

Sheriff Lance Beaufort wasn't the greatest talker in the world. But then, neither was Tim. They made awkward small talk. They talked about hiking trails in the area. Lance told Tim he'd lived in Mad Creek all his life, and he pointed out his various relations. He had a big family, and they were all stupidly good-looking and equally intense. All of them had blue eyes and black hair. Tim admitted he was an only child, but said no more about his less-than-Leave-it-to-Beaverish childhood. He was envious over Lance's big family, but they were also overwhelming, even from a distance. He was glad Lance wasn't as openly exuberant as his brothers.

Lance brought Tim a third beer and still didn't leave, standing closer to him than before. They ran out of things to say, so they just stood next to each other. It was comfortable, being quiet with Lance. And Tim was able to study him surreptitiously. Lance was a manly man. He had the shadow of stubble on his jaw even though he was clean-shaven, like his beard was so dark it was visible under the skin's surface. His black hair was neatly trimmed at the nape of a tan and attractive neck, and he had a small, dark birthmark on the tip of one ear. He seemed to get more attractive the more Tim looked. He had a kind of sexy glow. Sometimes Tim found Lance watching him with those blue eyes that seemed to speak more fluently than his mouth.

When that happened, the whole room got a little warmer. Honestly, the butterflies in Tim's stomach had pretty much started the moment he'd seen the sheriff approach and hadn't quit since. There was no denying Lance Beaufort was a very, *very* attractive man who hit all of Tim's buttons. But Tim was starting to feel more than an aloof appreciation of his looks, probably because Lance was showing him attention. It'd been a long time since Tim had felt interested in a man like this, a hopeful stirring of groin, brain, and heart. Maybe it wouldn't be so bad to be alone with Lance. Maybe.

When Lance still hadn't left his side through three beers and a dinner plate, Tim couldn't take it anymore. He was imagining all sorts of things about Lance Beaufort and those beautiful eyes. And he was setting himself up for a major fail if he was wrong. So he blurted it out.

"So… are you involved with anyone?"

Lance licked his lips and seemed unsure of the answer. "No. Not really."

"Oh. Are you gay?" Tim inwardly groaned. *Smooth. Way to ease into it.*

"I wasn't before."

What did that mean? Tim waited, but Lance said nothing more. "You weren't before, but you are now?"

Lance shrugged. "I don't think gender is that important."

"Really? Do you mean you're bisexual?"

Lance looked him in the eyes. "Yes. I guess that's what I am."

"Oh. Okay."

A frisson of excitement shot though Tim. So this was what it appeared to be. Lance wasn't just hanging out with him to be a good host. But did Lance really *like* him like him? If so, why? And would this go anywhere? There was probably at least a one-night stand in it. But even though Tim's anatomy was a hundred percent on board with the *idea* of having sex with the tight-bodied, strangely intense man looming next to him—he had a crazy urge to run his fingers through all that black hair—the reality of it made Tim hesitate. It wasn't so much that Lance

164

frightened him, the way some men did, but... he didn't really know Lance. And even if Lance wasn't cruel, what if it was just a one-night stand? Honestly, Tim couldn't face any more rejection.

He didn't move away, though, and neither did Lance. After starting his fourth beer, Tim didn't even question it. At some point, he realized most of the people had left. He and Lance were standing in the hallway to the bedrooms, each of them leaning back against an opposing wall, staring at each other across the space, saying nothing.

"You two still here?" Lily sounded both surprised and pleased with herself as she passed them. "'Scuse me. Bathroom."

"Oh. Wow. It's probably late." Tim blinked. How long had he been just standing there staring at Lance? Four beers was too much, clearly.

"I'll drive you home." Lance took Tim's elbow and steered him gently to the door.

"Good-night, Lily! Thank you!" Tim called out as he was herded from the house.

*   *   *

Lance was happy as he drove Tim home. Tim hadn't rejected his company at the party. In fact, there were tantalizing wafts of interest coming from him that had increased over the course of the night, small tells of arousal and curiosity. His hazel eyes had darkened to liquid brown. His earthy scent warmed and turned heady and musky. Lance had edged closer little by little, and Tim hadn't pulled away. Tim *liked* Lance. He liked him, as a man!

Then again, Tim was also more than a little drunk.

They pulled into Tim's driveway. Lance put the car in park but left the engine on. *Now what? Don't blow it.*

"Thanks for the ride." Tim rolled his head on the headrest to look at Lance. His hand was on the door handle, but he didn't seem eager to get away. He looked relaxed from the alcohol and… expectant.

The low-level excitement that had been running through Lance's body all night blossomed hot and heavy in his stomach. And suddenly it was achingly clear. Shit. He did. He liked Tim *that way*. He loved being with Tim, and now that he was in his human form, and Tim was looking at him all open and wanting, the affection slammed into physical desire so hard it was like a kick to the balls.

166

Lance swallowed. Should he try to… kiss Tim? Or…?

He hesitated too long, unsure what was best. Tim suddenly blushed, as if embarrassed, and opened the door. "Right. Good-night," he mumbled. He headed for the cabin, weaving a little.

Lance considered chasing after him, making sure he got inside okay, maybe trying the kiss after all. But was that the right thing to do? He knew he could be overbearing. The last thing he wanted was to scare Tim away, not when he'd made such progress tonight. So he just sat and watched while Tim let himself inside, closed the door, and turned on the lights.

Lance put the truck in reverse and pulled out. He paused at the end of the driveway, then turned right and continued up the hill to the lookout point at the top of Broad Eagle Drive. He hesitated, telling himself he shouldn't. But he couldn't resist. He took off his clothes and shifted. Soon he was at Tim's back door, barking and scratching on the wood.

"Chance!" Tim threw the door open. He'd already changed into his pjs. "Where've you been, buddy? Did you come earlier and I wasn't here? Sorry. I left the greenhouse door open and a bowl of food in there, but I guess you didn't see it."

Chance wove past Tim's flannel-covered legs, brushing his coat against them.

167

"I went to a party tonight. Can you believe it? This town is really nice. And guess who hung around me all night long and drove me home? The sheriff!" Tim looked at Chance with wide eyes, as if he expected him to respond. Chance gave an enthusiastic, thumbs-up of a bark.

"I know! Crazy, huh? God, he's so good-looking." Tim's happy, and somewhat drunken, retelling faded. A perplexed, worried look came over his face. He stared off into space. Chance barked.

"Come on, buddy. I need a snuggle."

Tim went into the living room, and Chance followed. Pretty soon Tim was lying on the sofa with Chance tucked against his side, the blanket over them. He didn't turn on the TV, seemingly content with whatever scenes were playing in his own head. He petted Chance idly.

"He didn't make a move or anything. But he did say he was bisexual. I wonder if he'll ask me out? I want him to but...." Tim sighed and snuggled closer to Chance.

But what? Don't stop there. Come on. Chance stared at Tim, panting and silently urging him to keep talking.

"I'd rather be alone forever than let someone hurt me

again." Tim spoke fiercely. Then he rolled his eyes. "God, I'm such a reject. You're not scared of anything, are you, Chance?" Tim rubbed Chance's ears with both hands and made an exaggerated pouty face.

It occurred to Lance that Tim wasn't talking about 'being hurt' the way most people meant it, getting his feelings bruised. He was talking about *being hurt*. A low growl erupted in Lance's throat. The idea of any man hitting Tim made Lance insane. Had there been someone else who did that, besides Tim's dad? Someday, Lance was going to find anyone who'd ever hurt Tim and bite their cowardly asses so hard they'd never be able to sit down again.

Tim laughed. "No one's hurting me right now, Chance. Chill."

Lance growled louder, upset.

Tim buried his face in Chance's chest. "You're right" came his muffled voice. "I can't go through life being held back by fear." He looked up, smiling. "Hey, maybe that's why you're in my life, huh? To teach me to take chances? I took one with you and look how great that turned out."

Chance licked Tim's face.

"I should jump all over Sheriff McHotty, right? Or at least throw myself in his path like a Victorian damsel. Assuming he ever comes around again."

Chance barked an affirmative. He was going to make sure of it.

*   *   *

It was nearly dawn. Lance's consciousness let go of the last fingers of a very pleasant dream. He stretched and smiled, his eyes still closed. He'd been dreaming about Tim, running after him in the woods on all fours, playing rambunctiously. Then he wasn't on all fours anymore, he was on two legs. He caught Tim, held him, pressed him tight against his throbbing erection. His whole body was on fire as he.... Mmm... pressed him close, rubbed.

Lance snuggled contentedly against the warm body in bed with him, lazily thrusting his erection against Tim's bare leg. Tim always slept in just his underwear and a T-shirt and his skin was warm and he smelled like heaven and—

Lance's eyes flew open. Fear and panic slicked through him like a flash flood.

He was in Tim Weston's bed. In his human form. Naked.

170

With an erection pressed up against Tim's leg.

Lance barely caught himself from leaping out of bed. No doubt he'd make a racket and wake Tim up. Right then Tim was deeply asleep, his face turned toward the wall, one hand up by his head, lightly curled.

Dear God. When Tim had gone to sleep, it had been with Chance curled up next to him. If Tim caught him here like this, what would he think? He'd think that Sheriff Lance Beaufort had broken into his home and gotten into bed with him naked and horny and uninvited. He'd think Lance meant to rape him. The very idea of Tim thinking that, of scaring Tim like that, made the gorge rise in Lance's throat, instantly quelling his desire.

Very quietly and very slowly, Lance pulled back from Tim. When he was finally free of contact, he slipped out of the bed. He didn't breathe again until he was on the other side of the bedroom door.

Heaving a shaky sigh of relief, Lance let himself out of the house, shifted into his dog, and ran all the way back to his cruiser at the overlook.

Once dressed, and safely inside, he sat behind the wheel, trying to calm down. He couldn't believe it. He'd shifted back to human form *in his sleep.* He'd come this close to ruining everything for good.

As the panic faded, Lance was left with a heavy feeling of sorrow. This was a wake-up call, a slap in the face that reminded him that what he was doing was more than ethically dubious. It was *wrong*.

There was no way around it. Seedlings or no seedlings, Chance had to disappear.

~10~

Puppy Bait

TIM WONDERED where he'd obtained the curse that was currently looming like a black cloud over his head. He couldn't recall offending any leprechauns or gypsy women. Or meeting any, really. Sure, he'd had a falling out with Marshall, but Marshall was more wiseass than wizard. He didn't have the mojo to wither the green thumb Tim had had since birth.

Or to cause his dog to abandon him. Or the hot sheriff not to call.

Two days ago, in sheer desperation, Tim had broken his carefully breadcrumbed budget to drive down to Fresno and purchase a new supply of vegetable seeds. They weren't even very nice varieties, just the ordinary sort you could pick up at Home Depot. But he didn't know what else to do. Two hundred dollars later, Tim had planted a whole new round of seed trays. Now he had to wait for *those*.

If these didn't come up, he'd truly lose his mind. Or maybe he'd already lost it. Tomorrow it would be a week since he'd last seen Chance, and he felt the dog's loss like a final, fatal blow. It was hard enough trying to keep his spirits up. He needed his best friend. And he was terrified something had happened to Chance. Was he lying hurt somewhere? Tim had called every vet in the area, but there were no reports of a black collie. He'd walked the nearby trail they'd hiked multiple times, calling for Chance. There was no sign of him. Had someone grabbed Chance and locked him up? Tim should have gotten a collar for Chance with his name and address on it. At least then, if Chance had another family he went to during the day, they might have called him to see what was up. But he hadn't done that. It was just another way he'd fucked up.

Tim used a small dibble to poke at one of the first seedling trays he'd planted. He couldn't even find the damn seeds, and he'd gone through three rows by now.

What the ever loving fuck?

There was a knock on the greenhouse door. Tim was so focused on his task that he jerked upright and gave a tiny, but still embarrassing, scream.

Sheriff Lance Beaufort stood in the greenhouse doorway,

wearing his uniform. Tim's heart made an effort to perk up and get excited about it. But he was just too low.

"Hey." He turned back to his seed trays with a sigh. "You don't have elves living around here, do you? Very spiteful, evilly sadistic elves?"

"Not to my knowledge." Lance came over and stood close to Tim—overly close, as was his wont. He watched Tim poke around. "Still no luck?"

Tim dropped the dibble. "I don't get it! I can't even find the seeds themselves. It's like someone just sucked them all out. I've never heard of mice or squirrels messing with seed trays. And even if they had, the soil would have been disturbed. I've seen nothing like that!"

Tim looked up at Lance, frustrated. Lance had a worried, thoughtful look on his face. "Hmmm. You don't—you don't know anyone who could be messing with you?"

"Like who?"

"I dunno. Someone you knew before? Someone who knows you're living here?"

Lance seemed to be implying something specific, but Tim didn't know what. The only people who knew he was here were

Linda and Marshall. Linda had no reason to mess with him. As for Marshall, he might wish failure on Tim, but to actually do something like this? He'd never be that clever or work that hard.

"I can't believe anyone I knew in Santa Barbara would drive all the way up here and dig up all my seeds. That's seriously weird. I guess it could have been an OCD rodent. I have no idea."

"Well." Lance cleared his throat.

Tim blushed. "Sorry. Don't mean to be so self-absorbed. Hi, Sheriff, it's nice of you to stop by. Unless you plan to arrest me or something." Tim laughed nervously.

"No." Lance took a step closer, which meant his uniform jacket and Tim's blue jean shirt were practically touching. "And it's Lance, remember? I wanted to see how you've been doing." He had worry lines around his frowning mouth, like he actually cared.

"Me? Sucky. My dog, Chance, has disappeared. He hasn't been back since last Saturday night. I'm afraid he's gone for good." Tim swallowed an invisible lump. It hurt more than Tim could express, but anyway, Lance didn't want to hear it. Tim knew most people wouldn't understand. Chance wasn't just a dog. He was special. Chance understood him more than any

176

person ever had.

"I heard about that. It's terrible to lose a dog." Lance sounded sympathetic. "My, um, my mom said she saw you at the grocery store yesterday and you were really upset."

"Yeah. She seemed upset about Chance going missing on my behalf. Almost angry. She's a character, your mom."

"Yes." Lance sighed, his intense blue eyes staring into Tim's. "I truly am sorry about Chance."

"Okay? It's not your fault, though."

"Well... I brought you something. Wait here."

Lance left the greenhouse. Tim wondered what it could be. Food? Maybe Lily made him a stop-being-suicidally-depressed casserole, one with a gazillion tons of fat and salt. His stomach grumbled in anticipation. He was way over mac and cheese and tuna.

Instead, Lance walked in with a puppy.

It was a very large puppy, though clearly quite young. It was black and white and tan, had long hair, and was so cute you could die.

"Oh my God!" Tim put his hand over his mouth.

"What…?"

"It's a mix but mostly Bernese mountain dog. It's a good breed for you. He can keep himself occupied in the yard while you work, but if you want to go hike, he's athletic enough for it. And he'll take all the cuddles you can dish out."

Lance held the dog out. Despite Tim's conflicted feelings—surprise, joy, doubt—he took the puppy. It licked his face with instant devotion.

"But… I can't take this. It's too much. Plus, I feel… I mean, I'm not ready to move on. Chance hasn't even been gone a week and… and he's my dog."

"Chance wouldn't want you to be alone," Lance said firmly. "And if he does come back, the two can keep each other company. Or if you can't handle both, I'll take the pup. That's no problem."

It was tempting, especially with both Lance and the puppy looking at him so hopefully. "Honestly, I don't even know where I'm going to be come September. If I can't get my produce business going, I'll be out on my ear. I shouldn't take a dog when I might end up homeless. He deserves better than that. He should find a forever home while he's still little and cute."

Lance stepped closer, his face sad and very serious. "Tim, that's not going to happen. You will never be homeless. We take care of our own here in Mad Creek."

Tim chewed his lip. "But what if I end up having to take a job in Fresno or Sacramento or something? I might not find an apartment that'll take a dog. And I'll be at work all day...."

The puppy wiggled in his arms, anxious, and Lance stroked his head, gently shhhing him. "You're worrying the pup. Don't fret. If for any reason you can't keep the dog, I'll make sure he finds a good home. He can always stay with me. Really. I want to do this for you. You need a companion."

That was sweet. Tim finally allowed himself to register the fact that Lance, Sheriff McHotty, had brought him *a puppy*. It was weird but also possibly the nicest thing anyone had ever done for Tim. He hugged the dog tighter. The puppy wasn't Chance, but his fur was baby soft and his pink tongue licked Tim's cheek eagerly. Tim wanted to say thank you, but his throat was thick and he was afraid he'd betray too much emotion if he opened his mouth. He loved Chance madly and nothing could ever replace him, but maybe there was room for this little guy too. Hell, *all* the dogs. Just bring him all the dogs. If he couldn't raise plants, maybe puppies would do.

Lance was watching him, and he seemed to know that Tim had relented. He smiled. "This dog here has a good heart. I picked him out especially for you."

"Oh? You speak dog?" Tim laughed, feeling more in control of himself.

"Yes," Lance said seriously.

Tim snorted. "I bet you do." He held the puppy up. "Man, you're heavy for such a pipsqueak. Are you going to be a big boy?"

Lance took one of the puppy's front paws and rubbed it. "He'll be big, but no bigger than Chance."

"How do you know Chance?"

Lance blushed. "You—you described him to me. Remember?"

Had he? Tim vaguely recalled talking about Chance at the party. He'd had four beers, so maybe he'd even run around on all fours and imitated the dog. Anything was possible.

"Oh. Okay. In that case, if you see Chance around? On your patrols or anything? Can you call me? Here. I have a picture." Tim pulled out his cell phone and showed Lance a photo of Chance. He was sitting in the backyard posing, his head tilted inquisitively. The image made Tim's heart ache.

Lance looked at it, his jaw set. "What a remarkably fine looking dog. I'll let you know if I see him."

Tim put away the phone. Then he realized Lance was standing so close he was half supporting the puppy. They were both holding and petting it. The two of them. Together. It was almost like a family or something.

Tim felt a rush of heat, which was predictable because, *hot guy*, but an equally strong surge of longing for that—a family. That was unexpected.

He brought me a fucking dog.

That was a nice man. Right? Someone with a good heart. But then, he'd already sensed that about Lance, despite his peculiar intensity. Or maybe because of it.

Tim made himself take his gaze off the dog and meet Lance's blue eyes. Lance was staring at him. A tingle went through Tim, right down to his toes.

"Oh," Tim said softly.

Lance leaned in and kissed him.

*   *   *

Lance could have planned this better. Maybe kissing Tim for the first time when there was a thirty-pound puppy between them wasn't the best idea. But Tim had looked at him so openly and hopefully and Lance couldn't hold himself back.

Tim apparently didn't mind. He opened his mouth immediately, deepening the kiss to a warm and sexy play of tongues. And when Lance tried to get ahold of himself and pull back, one of Tim's long-fingered hands slipped around his neck and held him in place.

Tim kissed him like he was starving to death, and all Lance could feel was joy at being accepted this way, as a man, as a lover. And all he could think was: *mine, mine, mine.*

The kiss stripped away the remaining tatters of his doubts and defenses, and Lance knew with certainly, by the swelling of his heart, that he had bonded with Tim completely. He was in love. He was a one-man dog, and Tim was it for him. At this point, he no longer cared what Tim was or wasn't up to. Lance would protect him to the bitter end, and that was all there was to it.

The puppy gave a little wiggle and a yip of discomfort. Tim finally let Lance go and leaned back.

"Wow," Tim said. His eyes had a sparkle Lance wanted to see there forever.

Lance swallowed. "Truer words."

Tim drew in a shaky breath. His pupils were dark and large, and he had a flush along his neck. Lance could sense how aroused Tim was, could smell the release of tantalizing pheromones and hear the tripping of his heart. It surged under Lance's own arousal, pushing it higher, and it called to every instinct in him. He wanted to herd Tim into a bedroom *right now*. And maybe that was broadcast on his face because Tim's eyes widened and he held up the ball of fur between them.

"Puppy!" he said with a nervous laugh.

Whether he was reminding himself or Lance was unclear, but Lance forced himself back from DEFCON 4. He didn't want to scare Tim. He leaned out of Tim's space. "Right. He's, um, he's a little uncertain because this is a new place. Best not leave him alone."

"Or scar him for life," Tim nuzzled the puppy's head. It was a comfort-seeking gesture, and Lance thought maybe Tim was a little unsure how far they should progress, despite his physical hunger. Lance reminded himself that Tim didn't know him, not really, not the way Lance knew Tim.

"Just wait til your mom sees him," Tim added.

"Oh. Well, it's best not to take him out in public until he's had all his shots. Bill McGurver has the little guy's records. He only needs his last set, and that's next week."

"Okay," Tim said agreeably. "But I'm sure your mom'll stop by sometime today. If not today, tomorrow."

A chill of pure ice ran up Lance's spine, killing his arousal. "What?"

"Oh, she's always coming by and bringing me food. She's been so generous. It's really helped with my grocery bill."

Fuck. Lance should have noticed. Those occasional nicer meals Tim had—chicken roll-ups with real chicken, a fresh green salad, a cherry pie. A cherry pie *like his mother made.*

Lance was suddenly furious that his mother had interfered like this, insinuating herself into Tim's home. But there was something else, something dark and horrifying just on the edge of his conscious mind.

"When... When was the first time she, um, came out here?

184

To the cabin. Was it just before the party Saturday night or...?"

"Oh, no! It's been a couple weeks," Tim assured him.

Lance felt the hair on the back of his neck stand up and his fingers curl inward. For the first time since he was a teenager, he felt like he might lose control, like his emotions were so wild he might give himself away without being able to help it. He was fighting not to bare his teeth. He had to get out of there.

"Lance? What's wrong? Did I say something?" Tim had gone pale.

Lance forced a grim, toothy smile. "No. I'll be back to check on you and the pup later."

Without explaining further, Lance turned on his heel and marched to his cruiser.

*　　　　　*　　　　　*

"Where are they?" Lance yelled as he stormed into his mother's house. He threw open her front door so hard, it crashed into the wall and left a dent.

His sister-in-law Nona, the baby on her lap, and her twin

boys playing on the living room rug, all looked up at him, mouths open.

"Um—" Nona said.

"Where is she? Do you have any idea what she's done this time?" Lance had never been more furious. If he were a car, he'd be venting steam from under his hood in a thick cloud.

"And… that's my exit cue." Nona got up smoothly. "Come on, kids. Let's go outside where there won't be any flying limbs." She added under her breath, "And I don't mean trees. Though no doubt, Granny deserves it."

Ricky and Randy protested that they really wanted to see flying limbs, and they never got to do anything fun, but Nona herded them out the door.

Lance found his mother at the kitchen table. Of course, she had to have heard his entrance, loud and irate as it was, but she sat there clipping coupons and looking perfectly calm.

"Well? Where the hell are they? You'd better goddamn tell me you didn't toss them out! Because I swear to God, Mother—"

"Oh, hush!" Lily said. "They're in the Franklin's greenhouse all snug and sound. And coming along nicely, I must say. The tomatoes are over two inches high!"

Up until this second, Lance hadn't completely believed it. He paced back and forth in the kitchen so... so flabbergasted and amazed and horrified, he was speechless. "I... I can't... How did... What the hell were you...."

His mother remained calm on the surface, clipping her coupons, but the scissors in her hands trembled and he could sense the tension in her body. "You said you were only going back to his house until the seeds sprouted. And I wanted to give you a little more time to... to get to know Tim. That's all. No harm done."

"NO HARM DONE?" Lance felt an overwhelming urge to destroy something. Ripping the cabinets off the wall would be a good start, though, ultimately, not helpful. "Do you have any idea how fucking upset Tim's been? He thinks none of his seeds sprouted! He thinks we have OCD rodents or fucking evil elves in Mad Creek! He thinks he's going to be homeless! He thinks he's a failure! How could you do that to him, Mother?" *How could you hurt my boy?*

Lily put down her scissors. She looked guilty and a little shaken. "Well. I didn't intend to hold on to them for so long. And it was really very clever of me, Lance. I got the same seed trays and the same potting soil and everything. Made a special trip to Fresno for it all. Gus and Wilson helped me move all the trays and swap all the little tray tags one day while Tim was at the market. They looked just the same, and all of them containing nothing but dirt!" She looked pleased with herself.

"Arg!"

"I only meant to leave them a few days. But then I could tell the two of you were getting along, that... that your dog was bonding with him. And then there was the party coming up—I couldn't have you giving up on Tim before that! And then the two of you were getting along so *famously* that night. I thought just an *eensy* while longer."

"Arg, arg!" Lance yelled, pulling at his hair.

"Lance, honestly, I didn't mean to upset the boy. I am sorry about that." His mother sniffed, her eyes going all sad and droopy. "But his plants are fine, really. You know Bev Franklin's a good gardener, and she's been taking care of them. Tim will be happy again when he gets them back, won't he?" She smiled tremulously.

Lance breathed in and out through his nose, in and out. Inside, his dog was howling.

He spoke through gritted teeth. "We're going to get those

plants back to Tim. And they'd *better* be all right. And then, once we have fixed the damaged you've done, we're going to have a long, long conversation about your meddling."

"All right," his mother said meekly. But Lance knew that puppies would grow bat wings and fly before anyone changed Lily Beaufort's fundamental nature. He *knew* that, and usually he stayed on top of her antics better than this, but Tim had been so distracting.

"Why on earth did you do it? What was all this for?" he demanded. "Why would you *want* me to bond with Tim?"

"Oh, honey." Lily got up and made Lance stop pacing. She took his hands in her warm ones. "He's the one for you."

Her eyes were so full of hope. Lance's chest hurt at the surety of her words. "You mean.... But he's a man," he said roughly.

"Well, it doesn't seem to bother you. And as you've pointed out, repeatedly, I have enough grandpups already."

"And he's a full-blooded human! You don't approve of intermarriage!"

Lily rolled her eyes. "You're always so black-and-white, Lance. I don't *prefer* it, because there's less of a chance of quickened children, as you well know, and I don't trust humans to be a spouse that's loyal and true. But I've accepted plenty of intermarriages in this community, haven't I? I just wanted the best for my own children. But you, Lance, you've always needed someone special. And... I knew it was right when I met Tim. He needs you too, so much."

Lance just looked at her helplessly, unable to say anything.

"Oh, my dear son." She squeezed his hands. "He makes you *dance*."

The words sent shivers down his spine. Lily. How could she make him want to rip apart the house with his claws one minute and make him weak in the knees with love the next? He hugged her to him, but it was a bit tight and she grunted loudly.

"I swear to God, if you *ever*...."

"Oh, hush," Lily said.

~11~
Public Disclosure

AT 6 o'clock the following evening, Lance knocked on Tim's door. When Tim opened it, thirty pounds of puppy charged out and jumped up on Lance like he was covered in bacon grease.

"Hey," said Tim. He looked a little nervous and very handsome in a white button-down shirt, navy cardigan, and nice jeans.

Lance's inner dog was wagging its tail so hard, he had difficulty keeping his hips still. There was no chance of reining in the grin that spread across his face.

"Oh, don't you two look handsome!" Lily came up behind Tim, her cell phone in hand.

"Mother—"

"Come on, boys! Tim, why don't you step onto the porch so I can get those nice trees for a backdrop? Put your arm around

191

him, Lance. There you go. Say 'puppy dog tails'!"

Lance gave his mother a flinty, warning smile. "Honestly, it's easier just to go along with her," he said through his gritted teeth.

"I've figured that one out," Tim muttered back.

"Now don't you worry about a thing, Tim! Stay out as late as you want. Renfield and I will be happy as clams."

"You be a good boy, Renny!" Tim rubbed the puppy's ears firmly and kissed his nose. Lance's ears twitched, remembering how nice that felt.

Lance's mother was watching him with a smirk, and he felt his face heat.

He walked Tim to the car and opened the passenger door. "Just give me one second. There's something I need to tell my mother."

"No problem," Tim smiled. "I'll just...." Lance waited for him to complete the thought. "Hang. Here. I'm good!"

Lance shut the door as Tim rolled his eyes at himself. He went into the cabin, smiling stupidly. It was sort of nice to see awkward Tim back again. It meant he cared what Lance thought, right?

"Is everything ready to go?" he asked Lily.

"Oh goodness. It's all arranged, Lance. Not a thing for you to worry about."

"Give me ten minutes at least to get down the hill."

"Yes, dear. Gus and Winston have everything loaded, and they'll bring it over when I call."

"And whatever you do, be careful with those plants. Do not drop the trays!"

Lily looked heavenward and sighed. "Nothing will happen to Tim's plants. My goodness. Your protective streak is turning into the Nile River over that boy."

Lance ignored that. "And don't forget Roman will be here around seven to check the plants, so try to have everything set up in the greenhouse by then."

"You know my opinion on that," Lily's scolded. "I think it would be a nice gesture of trust if you told Roman he wasn't needed. You know Tim's not growing any drugs!"

"I just want to finish this once and for all," Lance said firmly. "Besides, I mentioned it to Roman awhile back, and he keeps bringing it up. I think he's eager to use his skills, and I'd feel stupid telling him I changed my mind."

"If you say so," Lily said with a martyred sigh.

"He won't find anything, so no harm done. And remember, when we get back, neither of us is going to mention the plants. Just let Tim discover them in his own time. It's probably for the best if he finds them in the morning when we're not here." Although Lily was a consummate liar, Lance didn't trust her not to look obnoxiously pleased with herself. And Tim would be looking for some kind of answer as to why his seeds had turned into one and two inch plants overnight. Best if he and Lily weren't around as obvious targets of suspicion.

Lance would love to tell Tim what really happened, but that story made no sense without the concept that Lance equals Chance. And that was a little more strain than should be put on a first date.

"My, how you do go on," Lily said dryly.

"Yeah? Wonder where I got that from?"

"As if I weren't scheming long before *you* were born."

"Believe me, I'm aware. I'll keep Tim out until at least ten."

Lily's face smoothed into a knowing smile. "You stay out as long as you like. You two have a wonderful time!"

Lance huffed and headed for the door.

"Just relax and do what comes naturally, Lance. Even if you're a prude, your dog isn't. I know you have it in you!"

"Thanks for the vote of confidence, Mother."

"You're welcome."

*   *   *

As they drove down the hill toward town, Tim had the thought that this was the first actual date he'd ever been on in his life. Dillon, in high school, was more fuck buddy and video game opponent than boyfriend. He'd had a few gay bar hookups when he'd lived in Santa Barbara, but it was always a frustrating experience. His body lusted after the alpha males in the clubs, the rougher the better, but he always ended up with some frail-looking twink swapping hasty blow-jobs in the bathroom. He was too afraid of getting in over his head with an aggressive guy. And afterward, he'd hate himself for being a coward.

This, though, this was something new. This was a real man who was good-looking, still had all his teeth, wasn't married, was responsible, employed, and seemed genuinely interested in more than getting into Tim's pants for the night. Even better, there was a connection between them, some emotional undercurrent linking them, and it made Tim feel warm and tingly when Lance was next to him. He wasn't sure when that had happened or how, but it had been there at least since the party. He'd never felt this way before. Was it mutual?

Tim told himself not to get his hopes up, but they were already so far up there, they were like the speck of a helium balloon in a clear blue sky. If only he could get past this residual niggle of fear. Lance was so… masculine, authoritarian, intense. Tim told himself Lance would never hurt him, and he believed that, consciously. But deep down inside, there was a voice that refused to be optimistic.

You're alone in a car with him, at night. He could do anything to you. And why wouldn't he? You're weak, a loser.

Tim told the voice to shut the fuck up and stop being a killjoy.

"It's a nice night for a drive, so I thought we'd go to the Mountain Place," Lance said as they pulled onto Mad Creek's Main Street. "It's about forty minutes away. I hope that's all right?"

"Sure," Tim shrugged. "I'm not in a hurry. It was nice of

196

your mom to offer to puppy sit."

"She has her uses."

"It's awesome that she… that she doesn't have a problem with this." Tim gestured back and forth between him and Lance.

Lance gave him a warm look. "Lily has good instincts. Well, that may be going too far. She can have incredibly *bad* ideas, but she's good at reading people."

Tim thought that was a compliment.

A car trying to catch the end of a yellow light ran out in front of them, and Lance braked hard. He automatically reached over to place a hand on Tim's chest as if to secure him, even though he was wearing a seat belt. But at the sudden move, Tim flinched.

"Sorry," Tim mumbled, when Lance dropped his hand.

Lance didn't say anything, but Tim knew his reaction had been weird and he felt like there was a big, flashing "*L*" on his forehead. Lance was going to think he was a basket case. But Lance drove on.

Just before they left Mad Creek, there was a craft store on the right that was closed for the night. Lance pulled into the driveway and drove the car to the back of the parking lot near a

197

row of trees. He parked.

It was a lonely spot. Tim felt himself tense up again. A warning voice in his head said Lance was angry with him, that he was going to yell or worse. Tim wished he hadn't accepted the invitation to come tonight. He should have stayed home with Renfield. He should have—

Lance shifted in his seat and took one of Tim's clenched and stiff fists into his. His blue eyes were soft. "Tim?"

Tim let out a shaky sigh. "Yeah? Sorry, I don't know what's wrong with me. I guess it's just been awhile since I've been out. Or, ever. Like this I mean. It's not you, it's me. Just ignore me. It's fine." *Please ignore me. Please don't be mad or want to take me home.*

Lance ran his thumb back and forth over Tim's knuckles until his fist unclenched.

"I know it'll take a while for you to get used to me. You don't know me, really, and you're smart to be wary of people you don't know. But I just want to say this: I would never hurt you."

Lance spoke calmly and with unwavering conviction. Tim looked down at the gearshift, unable to maintain eye contact. "I know that."

"You *don't* know that, not yet, but in time you will. And I know it's easy for someone to say they won't hurt you, or to promise never to do it again, and then do it anyway. But I've never hit anyone in my life. That's not my way. Don't get me wrong—if someone were a threat to me or mine, I would do what I had to do. But I would never hit someone I know, someone I care about. Any more than… any more than Chance would have bitten you. Do you understand what I mean? When someone has my loyalty, they have it absolutely."

Tim took a deep breath. He made a decision to be honest, because maybe if Lance knew there was a reason behind this he wouldn't think Tim such a spaz. But Tim had to look out the windshield while he said it.

"It's not that I distrust you specifically. I know it's not normal, that most people don't hit other people. It's just… my dad did. He hit me. Out of the blue sometimes. I wish I could get over being jumpy about it."

Lance touched Tim's chin and gently turned his head so he was forced to look at Lance.

"Someday you will. Someday you will know, down in your deepest heart, that I would never lift a hand to you, that I would

199

protect you from anyone else who would try to hurt you with my dying breath. Until then, you won't scare me off or annoy me if you feel unsure. Okay?"

There was a thread of emotion in Lance's voice that was... *God...* more affection than Tim had ever heard directed at him in his life, more than he deserved. *Someday.* Lance saw a future for them. Tim wanted that future to be real.

He felt so much—gratitude for Lance's understanding, wonder at finding such a good guy, a desire to show Lance he believed him—that his tongue just quit in defeat. So instead of talking Tim clutched Lance's jacket with one hand, pulled him in, and kissed him.

*   *   *

Lance sank into the kiss, happy to have an excuse to touch. He'd wanted to touch Tim that night at the party, wanted to touch him when they'd kissed in the greenhouse, heck, longed to hold him close with two strong arms when he'd been lying next to him on the couch as Chance. And now, with his protective instinct aroused, there was no way he wasn't giving in to that urge.

He wrapped his arms around Tim and pulled him close. Tim came willingly and even helped by removing his seat belt and scrambling over the console. Somehow, between Lance's narrow hips and Tim's long, lean legs, they ended up with Tim straddling Lance's lap in the driver's seat. Good thing Lance liked to drive with his seat as far back as possible.

Tim kissed Lance for all he was worth, his tongue warm and soft. He tasted like sunshine and sweet earth, like boy and mate, like the essence of love and the swamping lust of sex. Lance had never been looking for a mate, but right then he couldn't imagine how life had any color without this right here— this living, warm creature in his arms.

Tim broke the kiss, and Lance pressed him even tighter so he could feel Tim from his shoulders to his lap. He buried his face in Tim's neck and breathed in the delicious heat. Tim's heady scent curled around his nostrils and soaked into his brain. It should have lowered the arousal level, going from a kiss to a hug, but it didn't. Having his mate this close, close enough to feel and smell and taste, was like having the most delicious morsel imaginable held just before his nose. Lance wasn't feeling disciplined enough to resist. But he didn't want to push

Tim either.

"Hey," Tim whispered, "I know we just talked about me being, well, wary of violence? But I want you to know there's another part of me that really wants you to push me up against a wall someday, *Officer*. As long as there's no actual pain involved, and you're not actually mad. It's just—you don't need to handle me like glass. I'd prefer it if you didn't."

"That so?" Lance felt another gush of heat in his groin at the images that conjured up.

"Yeah."

Tim wiggled closer, and Lance pulled him even tighter. The ridge of Lance's erection met the softness of Tim's sack while a throbbing heat pressed into his own stomach.

Tim groaned. "Oh my God. I feel that, and I want to touch it so much. I have zero will power."

"Saves me a lot of effort having to talk you into it then, because I don't have any either." God, no. His dog nature saw no reason to be coy about what he wanted or the fact that he wanted it immediately.

Tim leaned back so he could look at Lance. There was a red flush splashed across his throat, and his eyes were dark and dreamy. He bit his lip, uncertain. "Don't we have dinner reservations?"

"Nope. We'll get seated whenever we show up."

"Oh. Isn't it illegal to do stuff in a car in a craft store parking lot?" He smirked, teasing.

"I won't tell the sheriff if you won't," Lance said seriously.

In all honesty, being caught getting hot and heavy in a parked car with a man would make Lance a lifelong butt of jokes and/or piss townspeople off. But right then, Lance cared less about that than he'd ever cared about anything in his entire damned life.

"I see. You have the justification thing down, huh?" Tim cocked a sly eyebrow and trailed his fingers down Lance's chest. He popped a few buttons, teasingly, and seemed delighted at the dark hair that was revealed. He popped a few more and ran his fingers over Lance's chest with a mesmerized look.

"Oh, God. Your hair is so soft and so black. It's really hot."

Lance swallowed, not trusting himself to speak. He did have pretty thick hair on his chest, and he was glad Tim didn't mind. The pleasure of Tim running his fingers through it made his eyes go half-lidded and his dick throb.

Tim tugged on a small patch of white near his left nipple and grinned. "Getting old?"

In answer, Lance growled and thrust up with his hips.

That redirected Tim sufficiently. His eyes dropped down to Lance's lap and grew wide. His fingers brushed against the bulge in Lance's jeans, tracing its outline, then rubbing across it with his thumb. They both simultaneously groaned.

"Yeah," Tim panted, "self-control detonated, ka-blam. I know I shouldn't be this easy, but holy hell I want you."

"There's nothing easy about wanting someone this much," Lance growled, and he took the reins. His mate was aroused and aching and needed him, and by God, Lance would give him what he wanted.

He brought Tim back to his lips with a firm hand around his nape and kissed him more deeply than before, setting up a purely filthy rhythm with his thrusting tongue. He managed to undo Tim's button and zipper with one hand and pulled out his erection.

Mine.

"L-lance," Tim gasped. He fought to get Lance's pants open, and then his slender hand wrapped around Lance's thick shaft and it was—dear lord. Perfect.

Lance's concentration shattered, and he had to break the kiss, only able to put his forehead to Tim's chin, close his eyes, and hold on. He set a relentless pace, too turned on to tease, and Tim mirrored it. They liked the same moves, if the tensing in Tim's thighs and the hitching of his breath was any indication. But Tim felt better in his hand than Lance had ever felt to himself, hard and warm and *sex* and... and rutting and....

"*Lance.*"

"Got you."

"S-so crazy. *Fuck.*"

"Perfect."

It was, but it wasn't enough. Lance was dying to be able to bury his face in the richest parts of Tim's scent, to taste and touch him everywhere. But that wasn't possible in the car. For now they were on a one-way roller coaster that went up and up and up. Sooner or later—sooner if the tightening spiral in Lance's groin were to be trusted—they had to fall. Their hands moved in sync, Tim mouthed and panted and moaned at Lance's temple, and Lance's head spun with sensation—the sounds, the smells, and the erotic images that threatened to do him in when he dared open his eyes and look down. His mind was so entranced it was difficult to tell who was touching whom and who was feeling what.

"Mmm. So good. Close—" Tim choked out, vibrating all over.

"Now." Lance meant himself, that he was there, but they came together. It felt like the sensations they caused in each other were energy bands so interwoven there was no sending one off the cliff without the other being pulled along. Lance had never imagined anything like it.

Lance slumped against Tim, his body singing and his mind offline. His dog was *very* happy.

After a while Tim nudged him. "You too tired to drive to dinner? We could hit McDonald's."

Lance laughed and forced himself to sit up. "No way. I'm taking you out to a nice place. Can you reach the glove compartment? There are wipes in there."

They cleaned up, and Tim shifted over to the passenger seat. He seemed to be avoiding Lance's eyes, so Lance leaned in and nuzzled his ear.

"Consider that an appetizer. The main course will be when

I can get you into a bed. Or at least up against a wall."

"I don't know, obviously the public sex thing works for me," Tim teased.

Lance pulled out of the parking lot and groaned. "I see an impeachment in my future. Because *you* could talk me into anything. You could probably get me to have sex in the diner during the lunch hour rush."

"I swear to be responsible in the use of my super power," Tim said solemnly.

Just for that, Lance held Tim's hand the entire drive to the Mountain Place, even though he'd always been a stickler for ten and two.

Some things were worth breaking the rules for.

*   *   *

The Mountain Place was a small, cozy log cabin with an upscale home-cooked menu. It was Lily's favorite place to stop when they drove to Fresno for shopping. It wasn't overly fancy, but it felt more romantic than usual tonight. Maybe that was because they were seated near the roaring fireplace. Or maybe it was the way Tim looked, golden and glowing, in the firelight, the sharp boyish lines of his face softened. Or maybe it was the post-sex endorphins making Lance feel all mellow and smiley.

"So… how come you're not already married?" Tim asked as they waited for their main course. "You must be quite the catch in Mad Creek, especially if you date both men and women."

"You're the first man I've dated. And I haven't dated women much either."

Tim looked surprised. "Oh? Why not?"

Lance got as close to the truth as he could. "I'm very dedicated to my job. I figured it wasn't fair to marry someone and have children when I couldn't give a family the attention they deserved, when I had to put the town first."

"Oh." Tim's face fell, but he covered it quickly with a fake smile. "I get it. Married to your work."

Lance silently cursed himself. "No, that's not what I mean." He leaned forward, elbows on the table, and stared intently into Tim's suddenly shy eyes. "I'm explaining why I didn't marry a woman in the past. But… people change. I like you, Tim. And if you really want children, I… I'll support you as much as I can."

Tim looked shocked. He started to speak, swallowed instead, dumbfounded.

"Sorry," Lance drew back. Uneasiness pricked the hair on the back of his neck. He wanted to whine. "That was too soon."

Tim frowned. "Are you—are you jerking me around? You hardly know me."

Damn it. It was really hard to keep Lance and Chance separated and to remember that Tim's interactions with Lance had been so limited.

He was about to cautiously answer when the phone in his pocket vibrated. It could be an emergency call from his deputy, or it could be Roman. Lance glanced at his watch. It was 7:30. Roman then.

"Excuse me a minute."

"Sure."

Lance gave Tim an apologetic smile and stepped outside the restaurant's door to take the call. He felt a flush of nerves as he answered the phone.

What if Tim is growing drugs after all?

I don't care. I'll deal with it.

"Roman?" Lance answered.

"Hello, Sheriff. Reporting in, sir. I checked all the trays in the greenhouse. I also sniffed around the cupboards and bags in there."

"Yeah?" Lance felt like the future hung by a Damoclean thread, no matter that he'd told himself it didn't matter.

"It's clean. There's no trace of any of the plants I was trained to look for—no cannabis, no opium poppies, no mushrooms. They're just ordinary plants."

Lance felt relief wash through him followed shortly by a niggle of self-disgust. There had been nothing to it, ever. Then again, if he hadn't been suspicious, he never would have gotten to know Tim.

"Thank you, Roman. If you—"

"Hang on!" Roman's voice was suddenly tense. It sounded like he dropped the phone, and in the next instant there were popping sounds. Lance recognized them, with horror, as gunfire. They were accompanied by the sound of shattering glass.

"Roman!"

Shouting. More gunfire. Something large overturned.

Shit. *Shit!* It was difficult, but Lance forced himself to hang up so he could dial his deputy. He gave Charlie Tim's address. "Call in everyone we've got—now! I'll be there as soon as I can."

Dear God. Roman was at Tim's, and so was Lily. Lance had a horrible image in his mind of them lying near the greenhouse bloodied and dead, the furry heap of Renfield's body nearby.

Please, no.

Lance stalked back into the restaurant. The minute Tim saw his face he stood up. "Something's wrong?"

"I'm sorry, but we have to go."

"Of course."

Lance said nothing more, just threw money on the table and ushered Tim out. How was he going to explain this to Tim?

More importantly, what the hell was going on?

~12~
Massacre

SOMETHING WAS terribly wrong. Tim kept waffling between feeling scared about it and telling himself it had nothing to do with him, that it was some sheriff-related emergency involving people he didn't know. But even if that were the case, he was worried for Lance, because Lance was going to be in the thick of it, whatever it was.

Lance had been so unbelievably sweet and affectionate tonight—in the car when they'd fooled around, holding his hand on the drive, taking him out to a nice place, and what he'd said over dinner, implying they had a future. That was nuts! Tim had heard stories about people who knew they were going to end up with someone as soon as they met. He'd never believed something that romantic and momentous could happen to him. But there Lance had been, talking about supporting Tim if he wanted kids. And it was only their first date! Tim might have thought it was just a ploy to get in his pants, but Lance didn't

212

strike him as a liar. He didn't say much, or say it well, and what he did say seemed sincere.

Tim couldn't deny the thrill of being with a man that sure of himself, nor the undercurrent of emotion that ran between them. He wanted it to be for real like he'd never wanted anything before. What would it be like to share his life with someone? To have someone to come home to, someone to share his successes and failures with, to build a home with, a home that was safe from fear and violence. It sounded too good to be true.

Yup, it would be just like Tim's luck to meet the love of his life and have him killed in a shootout later that same night.

Lance hadn't said anything more about the phone call, but his jaw was tight and his hands were locked on the wheel as he drove fast. He even leaned forward a bit as if he could get them there faster that way.

Tim didn't want to distract him when he was so focused, but on the other hand, maybe he should say something supportive. "Is it work related or family? The emergency."

Lance pressed his lips together tighter. "I'm not sure. Can you do me a favor? Can you get my phone out of my jacket pocket and try to call the last person who called me? Just see if they pick up?"

"Sure."

Tim did as asked, fished the cell phone from Lance's pocket. The last call received was from 'Roman'. He dialed it. He let it ring a long time, then hung up, and did it again. "No answer."

Lance's mouth tightened, but he said nothing.

"Is there anything else I can do to help?" Tim hated seeing Lance this worried, and it was making him anxious as well.

"Listen—" Lance stopped himself, hesitating.

"Anything."

"When we get to your cabin, I'm going to need you to stay in the car. Can you do that for me?"

"*My* cabin?"

Lance nodded grimly, his hands clenched on the wheel so hard his knuckles were white. "Gunshots were heard there. But I don't know what's going on yet, so try not to worry. It could be nothing."

"Oh my God. Your mother is there. And Renfield!"

Lance nodded tersely.

"*My* house. Why would there be gunshots at my house?"

Tim was having a hard time getting his head around it, but he felt panic wake up and lift its head down deep in his gut.

"Keep calm. We don't know what's going on yet. But is there anyone... anyone who wishes you harm? Anyone capable of coming after you?"

"No!" The idea was preposterous.

"Not your father?"

Tim gave a bitter laugh. "He can hardly make it to the store for smokes. Besides, he wrote me off long ago. He has no idea where I am."

"Anyone else? What about—"

"What about what?"

Lance looked conflicted, which just confused Tim more. "I don't know. No one's contacted you since you got here? Someone you didn't want to know you were here?"

Tim couldn't help feeling that Lance was referring to someone specific. The only person that fit the bill was Marshall. "Why? Did someone call the sheriff's department about me? If my ex-boss did, he's off his rocker. I'm not growing any of the hybrid vegetables I made for him. He's a doofus."

"Would this Marshall be capable of violent retaliation?"

"What? No!" Tim couldn't imagine it. "Marshall runs an organic produce business. He's a douchebag, and a liar, and a cheat. But... no. He'd be too afraid of his reputation to do anything illegal. He's more the type to lawyer you to death."

"All right."

Tim tried to imagine what else could have happened. "Maybe it was just hunters who were shooting near the cabin? It might not have anything to do with me at all."

"Maybe," Lance said, but his agreement didn't make Tim feel any better.

*   *   *

When Lance pulled into Tim's driveway, there were three police cruisers already there. His deputy, Charlie, had called when they were still ten minutes out, so Lance knew what to expect. He hadn't found the words to tell Tim.

"Oh my God," Tim said at the sight of the flashing lights. Even in the dark, there was enough light to see that the front of the cabin was shot up, the windows blown and bits of wood and glass on the porch where bullets had hit the logs. "Oh my *God!*"

"Tim, remember what I said, I need you to stay in the—"

Tim opened the passenger side door and, before Lance could grab him, took off running toward the house. Lance cursed and threw the car into park and went after him.

On the phone, Charlie had said the perps were gone, but Lance was still worried. Until they'd done a full sweep of the woods in the area, they couldn't be sure. And the idea of Tim being exposed to a sniper was terrifying.

Lance caught up to Tim where he was standing frozen, staring at the cabin. Tim was a little taller than Lance, but Lance did his best to wrap his arms around Tim protectively from behind, becoming a living shield and offering grounding comfort at the same time. Charlie came up to them.

"Sheriff! It looks like there were at least three shooters, and they were in a truck. I put out an all-points, but the only description we have of the truck is from your mother, and she didn't get a good look."

"Was it black? I have reports of a suspicious black truck in the area. Roman got the plates."

"No, sir. It was silver. Lily is sure of that."

"Was anyone hurt? What about Roman?"

"No one was hurt, no sign of blood. But there's a shitload of property damage. Pardon my French. And we haven't seen Roman. His truck isn't around either."

Charlie looked at Lance pointedly, obviously not wanting to say too much in front of Tim. But between the lack of blood— *thank God*—Roman's truck being gone, and the look Charlie was giving him, it was likely Roman followed the shooters.

So far, Tim had been stiff in Lance's arms. Lance was still essentially wrapped around him, not even caring how it would look. But just then Renfield came trotting around the corner and Tim broke free and ran toward him.

"Renny!" Tim bent over and picked up the pup. "Thank God you're okay. You're shaking! Was it scary?"

Despite Tim's attempt to soothe the dog, his own voice was too high and sounded false to Lance's ears. He was in mild shock.

"Lily's okay?" Lance asked Charlie quietly while he had the chance.

Charlie replied in a whisper. "Lily changed and took off

into the woods when she saw the shooters. She kept the puppy with her. She's fine. As for Roman, we found his clothes in the back of the cabin. But his truck's gone now too, so he must have shifted back to human." Charlie's teeth bared, his lips pulling back. He was territorial when it came to the sheriff's department and jealous of the work Roman had been doing, though he'd never said as much directly. "Probably got scared and took off."

Lance shook his head. "Roman's a good man. If he's not here, he must have gone after the shooters." Lance started to move for Tim, but Charlie held his arm.

"One more thing. Lily said she heard them shouting after they shot everything to hell and back. They said 'No one grows pot around here but us. Get the fuck out or next time the bullets will be for you.'"

Lance gaped. "But... Roman told me on the phone there weren't any pot plants!"

Charlie shrugged. "We looked around. Didn't see anything like that. Think it was a case of mistaken identity?"

An idea tickled Lance's brain, as horrifying as the worst nightmare he'd ever had, the kind where you've done something wrong, and when you wake up, you're relieved and grateful that it wasn't true. But nothing was going to wake Lance up this time.

219

He looked up to check on Tim. Tim was gone.

*   *   *

Tim stood in the greenhouse holding Renfield. His whole body was numb, and his arms were about to give out under the weight of the heavy pup, but he couldn't let Renny down. There was glass everywhere.

Someone, some crazy-ass malicious bastard, had shot out every pane of glass in the greenhouse. Glass shards and glass powder were everywhere. But as crazy and violent as that was, that wasn't what Tim was staring at.

In the greenhouse, among all the broken glass, shot up bags of dirt, and overturned stools, were his seed trays. All of them had been knocked or hurled off the tables, their large plastic frames wrecked among the spilled dirt. But even that wasn't what Tim was staring at.

He was staring at the plants.

Among all that debris were dozens, hundreds even, of small green plants. They'd all been knocked out of their dirt homes, fine baby roots exposed, leaves starting to wilt, stems snapped. There were young tomato plants and peppers, melons and the serrated leaves of strawberries, broccoli and radish seedlings. And roses. There were dozens of rose plant starts lying exposed among the dirt and glass.

Tim stared, unable to make sense of any of it. Renfield whined and licked Tim's face and only then did Tim realize he was crying.

"Tim?"

Tim turned, as slowly and stiffly as an arthritic octogenarian. He saw Lance and his mother in the doorway.

"I don't understand." Tim's voice sounded very far away, like he had cotton balls in his ears.

Lance and his mother exchanged a guilty look. Lily looked especially ashamed.

"What? What did you do?" Tim asked her, a curl of dread making him nauseous.

Lily said nothing. She couldn't meet his eyes, instead looking down at the floor.

Oh. Oh, no. Through the disbelief and the shock, something hot and hideous bloomed. Tim was suddenly afraid this was going to be bad. It already was horrible, but it was worse than that. It was Carrie-and-the-bucket-of-blood bad. He'd been *had*, hadn't he? He'd been played in some awful, soul-crushing way.

"What's going on?" Tim asked Lance, louder now.

Lance flushed red and looked embarrassed. "I think… three men came and shot the place up. They thought you were growing pot. It was meant as a warning."

"What?" Renfield wriggled in Tim's arms, and he just couldn't hold him anymore. He walked to Lily and shoved the puppy at her. "There's glass everywhere. Don't let him down."

"I won't," she agreed quietly.

Tim turned to Lance, hands now on his hips. "Why the hell would anyone think I was growing pot?"

Lance swallowed and looked at Tim's chin. "I thought you were." His voice was halting. "I thought that at first. There's been trouble with marijuana growers in the nearby county, and I wasn't sure what you were going to be doing out here. At first."

Tim couldn't believe what he was hearing. "So… what? This is your fault? You spread rumors about me?"

Lance finally met his eyes, but he was frowning. His eyes were sad. "I don't know, Tim. It's not like I went around telling

222

people, but...."

"Great! Thank you. I appreciate that." Tim said bitterly. "Now can someone explain why my fucking plants are lying all over the greenhouse floor? Plants that were missing up til now? I mean, what the actual fuck?"

Tim waved at carnage on the floor. The sight of the young plant massacre broke his heart. All that work. All that money. All that time he thought he was crazy, or that he'd lost his ability to raise so much as a spot of mold. But the plants had grown, somewhere, somehow, and returned only to be destroyed. It was a gigantic slap in the face.

"How could someone...?" His words choked in his throat.

"Tim, you have no idea how sorry I am. Maybe we can salvage some of them." Lance's voice trembled with emotion.

Tim spun on him. "You did this! You thought I was growing pot so you stole all my seed trays. You... you made me think.... Oh my God." Tim put his hand over his mouth. He was going to be sick. A black pit opened beneath his feet. The betrayal was all the worse because he'd started to trust Lance, he'd started to care for him.

"It wasn't like that," Lance said, raising his hands up

imploringly. "I swear."

"It was me," Lily said abruptly. "I took the plants. I didn't mean any harm, Tim. I just wanted you to spend more time with Lance. I always meant to put them back safe and sound."

The pair of them, they were both completely insane, demented loons that somehow ran this town. Tim's chest was tight, and he couldn't breathe. He couldn't stand it one more second.

"Get out," he said. "Both of you. Get out of here and don't ever fucking talk to me again!"

"Tim, please." Lance's eyes were wet now, but that just made Tim hate him more.

"Get out! And take Renfield with you! I can't take care of him anyway since I'm now homeless. And I don't want anything you gave me, now or ever!"

It was an empty gesture given the fact that every window in the greenhouse was shot out, but nevertheless, Tim pushed Lily and then Lance through the open doorway and slammed the greenhouse door shut. Renfield wriggled in Lily's arms and cried, wanting to go to Tim. It broke Tim's heart, but then it was already broken. He held firm.

"Go on, leave! Now!"

"Please let us help clean this up," Lance said, his voice wrecked. "It's the least we can do."

"No, don't you get it? I can't stand to see your face! Just go! Please! And take your fucking Nazi police force with you!" Tim was so upset, he was shaking all over and he had to turn away from the doorway and grasp the edge of a table to keep his knees from buckling. So he didn't see Lance and his mother go. But he heard the cars driving away, and then, quiet. In the distance, there was a mournful, gut-wrenching howl. Even the wildlife was having a bad night, apparently.

Tim sank down on a clean patch of greenhouse floor and cried. But there was only so much crying a grown man could do, and after a while the parental urge in Tim surfaced, and he couldn't abide the sight of all those young plants on his greenhouse floor, exposed to the air like gasping fish.

He dug a pair of gloves out of a drawer and started to work.

225

~13~
Rescue Dogs

THERE WAS no sleep for Lance that night. He went back to the station and wrung every detail he could from the officers who'd been on the scene and the ones who'd gone out looking for the shooters. No one had heard from Roman.

It was all his fault, and Lance knew it. Everything bad that had happened to Tim since coming to Mad Creek could be laid squarely at the door of Sheriff Lance Beaufort.

The fact that none of his plants germinated.

The fact that his dog Chance had gone missing.

The fact that a fucking drug cartel had shot up his property and ruined what was left of his dreams.

The target of shame for all of it was on Lance's forehead. Or maybe on his heart.

He couldn't figure out where it had all gone so horribly

wrong. Each step along the way had *seemed* reasonable at the time. He was just doing his job making sure the suspicious new resident wasn't growing drugs, he'd had no cruel or malicious intent. And the Chance thing—yeah, that had definitely been iffy. Lance could admit now that there'd been a part of him, even at the very beginning, that had been attracted to Tim and wanted an excuse to spend time with him. Then his mother—Lance should have cottoned on to that little trick of hers long before he did. It wasn't like he'd blabbed around town about suspecting Tim of growing drugs. There'd only been that call to Sam Miller in Fresno. And he'd told Roman. And, dear God, his mother. Hell.

A dozen threads of reasonable—okay, mildly questionable—choices had led to disaster for Tim. Lance had never felt worse about himself in his life.

The thing that really hurt was that he loved Tim, and he only wanted to make things better for him. It had taken Lance so long to find someone he wanted in his life. Now that relationship was ruined.

But it wasn't in Lance's dog nature to wallow. It was his nature to *do*.

He had to fix this, whatever it took.

Lance fell asleep at his desk around five in the morning. He woke up to the sound of someone clearing their throat.

He sat up abruptly to find Roman standing in front of his desk in military posture, feet spread, hands behind his back, chin up. Lance could sense the emotions running high in him—excitement, determination, and simmer of anger and regret.

"Sorry to wake you, sir." Roman's gaze remained locked straight in front of him.

"No, I'm glad you're here. I was worried about you."

"I was out of communication because when I shifted into my dog form I left my phone behind."

"I figured as much. We found your phone in the greenhouse."

Roman clenched his jaw. "Yes, sir. I wanted to say—I'm very sorry, sir."

"Sorry?" Lance blinked, still trying to wake up. "What do you have to be sorry for?"

Roman hesitated, a slight frown the only thing that betrayed his turmoil, but Lance could smell it on him. "It was my

228

job to protect the town, and I failed."

Lance growled, low in his throat. "Jesus, Roman, it's wasn't your job to protect the town. It was mine."

"But you delegated the drug watch to me, sir."

"You were to patrol, nothing more. And you did warn me about those strange men you saw. Lily said the shooter's truck was silver, but was it them?"

"Yes, sir. One of the shooters last night was a man I'd seen previously in the black truck."

"Well, see there? You spotted them. I was the one who said we couldn't do anything about them until they did something illegal."

Roman hesitated. "Yes, sir. But I should have been able to stop the damage they did."

"There were three men with guns. You would have gotten yourself killed. You did the right thing, Roman. Now tell me what happened last night."

So Roman did. He'd been in the greenhouse on the phone with Lance when he heard the gunfire.

"My first thought was for Lily and Renfield. They were in

the house and the only ones on the premises by then. I didn't have a gun on me, only a Bowie knife. But I got out my weapon and approached the house. I saw the shooters, but they didn't see me. There were three of them and they were firing at the house. Then they started walking toward the greenhouse. I saw Lily in her dog form and Renfield slipping into the woods, so I knew they were safe. At that point, I... had to make a call."

"We found your clothes near a back window of the cabin."

"Yes, sir. I didn't think I could stop them without a gun, but I hoped I could track them. I knew they couldn't harm anyone with Lily and Renfield out of the picture. But I am sorry, sir. I suppose Mr. Traynor was very upset at the damage."

"It's broken glass. It can be fixed. Go on."

"I changed into my dog form and ran around the side of house. They saw me, but since I didn't attack them, they ignored me. I noted the details of their truck while they were shooting up the greenhouse. I have the license plate number."

"Excellent."

"Fortunately, I'd parked down the road, in case you and Tim came back and you didn't want him to see me. I ran to my truck, changed back to human, and prepared to follow them. The man from the black truck knew my vehicle from that day at the viewpoint, but there was nothing I could do about that."

"No. I suppose you had spare clothes in the truck?"

"Yes, sir."

Lance nodded, relieved he didn't have to imagine Roman driving around the county nude. "Go on."

"When they pulled out of Tim's driveway, they were going fast. I followed them down the hill, hanging back and keeping my lights off. They didn't see me." An expression of disgust crossed Roman's stoic face. "In fact, they didn't spot me the entire time driving down 41. Their truck wove a little. They might have been high, or maybe just goofing off. If they'd been paying attention, they would have spotted me."

"I'm sure you were very good at not being seen."

"I tried, sir. I followed them all the way to Coarsegold. They pulled onto a dirt lane so I parked my truck and changed. I followed them on all fours."

"Good work, Roman. And?"

"There's a compound outside of Coarsegold. An old house back off the road. I saw four vehicles and smelled at least five men plus the three that did the shooting. In the back, they had acres of cannabis. Pine trees hide the place from the road, but it ought to be visible by helicopter."

Coarsegold was over an hour away, well out of Lance's area of concern. He was glad the cannabis farm wasn't any closer. But even so, he'd report it. "Can you find it on a map?"

"Yes, sir."

Lance got up from behind his desk and went over to clap Roman on the shoulder. "Excellent work, Roman. We're lucky to have you to help protect this town."

Roman's Adam's apple bobbed as he swallowed. "Thank you, sir."

What Lance could feel pouring off him now was gratitude and affection—the start of a true pack bond. Lance felt a sense of satisfaction about that. But whatever he'd done right with Roman, it was nothing compared to the wrong he'd done to Tim. Tim, the human that he loved.

*   *   *

Tim worked until one o'clock in the morning. Fortunately

232

the light bulbs in the greenhouse ceiling were high enough to have escaped the carnage, though their light felt harsh and accusatory glinting off all the glass.

He swept aside the worst of the shards but then left them on the floor, focusing his efforts on the plants. Many of them were broken and damaged beyond salvation, but he cleaned out several seed trays, filled them with potting soil he scraped off the greenhouse floor, and replanted everything that looked like it might possibly survive. He watered them with $H2O$ and gut-felt prayers.

The young plants had been healthy and sturdy before the shooting. Someone had taken good care of them. But the fact that they were *his plants*, and someone had taken them and kept them from his care, continued to make him furious and hurt every time he thought about it. It was so bizarre, so hard to believe. What was *wrong* with Lance and Lily?

He should have known. Any guy who was that good-looking and a) was single and b) had essentially proclaimed his devotion on their first date, had to be completely mental. No wonder Lance hadn't been snatched up before now. And Tim had wanted it all to be true so badly!

Soft, wounded thoughts swirled in his brain like a

background dirge as he tapped down tender roots and crafted tiny splints for wobbly stems. He ignored the blood on his fingers from the all-but-invisible slivers of glass that dusted everything.

When he fell into bed that night, mentally and physically exhausted, he had a terrible nightmare about being hunted and attacked by a pack of dogs. Their teeth were made of glass.

*   *   *

When Tim woke up the next morning, it was to the sound of large machinery. Before he was fully awake, he thought it was a garbage or delivery truck in Marshall's moderately upscale neighborhood. Then he remembered he wasn't in Santa Barbara anymore; he was in Mad Creek.

He sat up abruptly. Whatever was going on, it was happening on Linda's property. A surge of anger had him out of bed and tugging on jeans and a sweatshirt. God damn insufferable, interfering people! What did it take to get them to leave him alone?

He pushed out the back door to see a tractor in his field turning the sod in the bright morning light. It was going over the pathetic bit he'd done himself and making it look like a real plowed field. There were half a dozen people in the greenhouse, cleaning apparently, and a man in white overalls was on a ladder measuring the broken greenhouse windows.

Tim stood there for a moment, taking it in. He was angry, but... well... if they were going to do a bunch of labor for him, he wasn't so proud he'd force them to leave. He'd sunk too low not to take any handout he could get. In fact, gratitude was making a sly move on the outside, creeping up on him— especially at the sight of that beautiful, ground-churning tractor. Still, he crossed his arms and glowered.

"I brought you coffee." Lance appeared at his side and handed Tim a large drink from the little coffee shack in town. It smelled like a mocha, a treat Tim loved but could rarely afford. Lance had Renny on a leash. The puppy immediately jumped up on Tim's legs, his tail going like a rotor blade. He looked so fucking happy.

Tim could ignore Lance, but the puppy? Not a chance. He bent down and scratched Renny's ears with his free hand. "You should learn not to jump up," he told the pup. "Guess your new owner will have to teach you that."

Tim refused to look at Lance, or drink from the fragrant

cup he held, even though he wanted the coffee badly.

"Listen," Lance said, in a soft voice. "I know you're angry with me, and I don't blame you one bit. But we're a community here, and we're not going to let you deal with this alone. I'm taking care of the greenhouse windows and the broken ones in the cabin too. They'll be installed tomorrow. Lily's got a clean-up crew working, and your field will be plowed and compost mixed in, donated by Grovener's. It's organic, so they say. And Ruth at Franklin's greenhouse sent over a bunch of her vegetable seedlings that are about the same size as yours were. Plus, you can order more seeds from wherever you prefer to get them and the expense will be covered."

Tim had to look up at Lance then. He was still hurt, deeply, and it hurt him more to look at Lance's handsome face, to remember what role he'd thought Lance might play in his life. Tim knew he should refuse Lance's help. But it wasn't like he had any other resources. And taking it didn't mean he had to be gullible to Lance or his mother again, right?

"Thank you," Tim forced out at last. "I do appreciate the help. But this doesn't mean I forgive you."

"I know. I want to explain more, but I'd rather wait until this is done and... and you're not so vulnerable."

If I'm vulnerable, it's your damn fault. Tim didn't say it, but he frowned harder. "This is all for nothing. When Linda finds out what happened, she'll probably kick my ass out anyway."

"Well, she doesn't have to know about it. The greenhouse will be better than it was before, and I have a guy working on the wood chips in the logs out front. He says he can patch them up so you'd never know they were there."

"But I *should* tell her," Tim insisted. *I'm not dishonest like you.*

Lance flushed, as if reading his mind. "Okay. That's fine. I'm happy to talk to her as the sheriff and let her know it was a case of mistaken identity and that you've gotten everything cleaned up. We can make it sound like it was no big deal."

Tim swallowed, thinking that was pretty solid of Lance, even though it didn't change his mind about trusting him. He watched the tractor cleave through the middle of the field. A dump truck carrying what looked like good, rich compost backed up close to the edge of the field and made a mountain of shining black gold. Wow. That shit was expensive.

For the first time since they'd pulled into the driveway the night before, the pain in Tim's chest eased a little. Maybe… maybe he would survive this after all.

"I saved some of the plants. Maybe a quarter of them," Tim admitted. It seemed like he should offer something since Lance was doing all this.

"I saw them in the greenhouse. Ruth said they looked like they were going to be okay. That's good. That's *really* good." Lance sounded stupidly relieved. But Tim wasn't ready to hear it.

"I'd better go help," he said stiffly. He started for the greenhouse, the untouched mocha still clenched in his hand. He'd get out of Lance's sight and drink it. Why waste a perfectly good mocha?

"Do you want me to leave Renny with you?" Lance called after him.

Tim looked back and saw both man and dog poised and staring at him with equal expressions of devotion and *let-me-in-ness*.

"Renny can stay for now," Tim said coolly.

As for Lance, that remained to be seen.

~14~
Chance Makes a Stand

LANCE WAITED three days to go and talk to Tim. He waited until the glass, shiny and new, was installed in all the windows. He waited until Ruth, Gus, and Lily had helped Tim plant several rows of peas and lettuces in the field and dozens of new seed trays in the greenhouse. He waited until the chips in the cabin wall were plugged, and the last crumbs of disaster had been swept away.

He had one shot at this. He wanted the hurt of all that damage to have faded.

He was also scared out of his ever-loving mind.

"Pfft! Just sweep him up in your arms and take him to bed." Lily had advised. "Lick your way out of it. Always worked on your father."

Lance had groaned and cringed at the illusion to parental

239

sex. Nope. Mental pictures unwelcome, thanks. But in all honestly, he'd do it if he thought he could get away with it. No, Tim would need an apology before he let Lance touch him again—if he ever did. And Lance knew he owed Tim some serious groveling. Licking wouldn't cover it.

Tim didn't look happy to see Lance when he opened the door.

"I brought two chicken dinners from the diner," Lance said, holding up the bag. "I'd really like to talk to you, so I'm hoping you don't make me eat mine in the car."

The joke fell flat, or at least Tim didn't respond to it. After a moment, he stepped back from the door. "Come in."

Tim walked to the kitchen, not checking to see if Lance was following or not. He put a piece of aluminum foil back on a casserole dish, as if he'd just been preparing to have it for dinner. He stuck it into a crowded fridge. "I can't even eat all the food people have been bringing by," Tim said in a neutral voice. "I froze some of it."

"That's good." Lance knew Lily felt almost as bad as he did, and she'd been the master of cooking-as-a-form-of-apology since time immemorial.

"So what do you want to say to me?" Tim asked bluntly, turning to give Lance a challenging look and folding his arms defensively.

"Do you want to eat first?" Lance put the bag on the counter.

"Not really. I don't care to eat with you right now. I'd rather just get this over with."

Despite his tough words, Lance could sense an undercurrent of want that radiated in Tim's being. He was like a mistreated junkyard dog snarling at anyone who approached, but at the same time wanting kindness so bad he ached with it.

The thought gave Lance a modicum of courage. "Okay then. I want to explain what happened."

"I know what happened."

Lance shook his head. The motion came out more exaggerated than it should be. His nerves were getting the better of him, and, inside, his dog paced anxiously. He pushed it down. "You don't know my side of it. I know I can be intense, and bullheaded, and protective as hell. And I'll admit I didn't handle things as well as I should have. But I never meant to hurt you."

241

Tim snorted. "Hard to believe someone could be that effective at something they didn't mean to do."

He had a point. Lance sighed. "Will you listen?"

*   *   *

Tim had done a shit load of forgiving people and believing them when they said they hadn't meant it. A lifetime of it. So he was determined not to be a fool now even though he wanted to be one. He wanted to forgive Lance and be held again in those arms, and believe, even if only for a short while, that someone loved him. He wanted to roll over because of all the work and goods and food people had donated to help him out. He hadn't paid for any of it, and he figured most of that had come out of Lance's pocket.

But he knew what that road was like. His dad could be charming and repentant too. His father had bought him 'blood presents,' as Tim thought of it, as if money could make up for broken bones. Further down the line, there'd only be more lost tempers, more pain, more apologies, and more grand gestures. And so it would cycle on. He'd promised himself he wouldn't live like that, always waiting for the bad shoe to drop.

"Go on and talk," Tim said, steeling himself to take anything Lance said with a huge grain of salt.

"Can we sit down?"

"I'm good." Tim preferred to remain on his guard.

Lance nodded, accepting it, and wiped a hand over his brow.

"The first time I saw you in the diner, you were asking about potting soil and gardening supplies. And... and you smelled like pot. See, there's been a lot of trouble in these mountains with marijuana growers. There was a shoot-out that killed three people a few months ago down near Merced. So I've been on the lookout. I don't want that shit in my town."

Oh God, the hitchhiker Tim had picked up. He'd reeked of the stuff. Tim said nothing.

"So... after the diner, I decided to follow up on you. See what you were up to, a routine check. That's when I visited you that first day, and you were in the greenhouse, and you shut the door like you didn't want me to see what was inside."

That day came back to Tim. *The rose hips.* He inwardly groaned.

"And you told me your name was Timothy Traynor. But when I did a routine check with Linda Fitzgibbons, she said she was renting the place to a Tim Weston."

"Oh God." Tim stumbled to the little table in the kitchen and sank into the chair.

Lance waited, not saying anything.

"My name is Weston. It was a stupid, impulse decision to say 'Traynor'," Tim admitted, feeling like a fool. "I'd just quit my job in Santa Barbara, and my boss was a real dick. I didn't want him finding me. Traynor is my mother's maiden name."

"All right," Lance said calmly. "Anyway, by that point, I had some reasonable concern that you might be up to something. So I called the police in Fresno. There's a drug squad guy there I'd met at a training session. I had him run a background check on you."

Lance's voice was bitter, and Tim looked up.

"I think the rumor that you were growing pot had to have leaked from that guy or at least from his office. There must be someone there who's on the payroll of the drug cartels. That shouldn't have happened, Tim. And I can't begin to tell you how sorry I am about it. But I'm going to find out how it got leaked, I promise you that."

Tim nodded. What Lance said made sense, and he seemed angry about it. But Tim still felt pretty much numb. "Fine. Is that all you have to say?"

Lance sighed. "Hell no." He wiped his face again, looking haggard. His hand absently drifted to his ear and scratched at it. Tim waited.

Lance suddenly let out a growl that was so deep it sent a prickle up the back of Tim's neck. "I had no idea my mother took your seed trays! I couldn't believe it when I found out! That was so far over the line.... But she didn't mean to hurt you either. You see she... she thought I would... well, I'd told her that once your seeds were up, and I could verify that they weren't pot, I wouldn't need to... to come by here anymore. Or, uh, concern myself with you. She was trying to set us up, Tim! She figured as long as I didn't know for sure what you were growing...." Lance huffed as if frustrated. "As soon as I realized what she'd done, I made her bring the trays back. That's why I took you so far out of town to dinner, so she had time to replace everything. It would have been fine! But then the shooters showed up.... And I'm.... Everything got... And it's my fault, ultimately. And I'm sorry!"

Tim blinked, trying to catch up. Lance looked so sincere, but what he was saying hurt. So the whole point of that date had been to get him out of the house so Lily could sneak back in the plants she'd stolen from him? Great. Perfect. Tim had had sex with Lance *in the car*, and believed all his bullshit talk. Lance really was an asshole. And even his answer about the seedlings didn't hold water. The past few months flashed through Tim's mind.

"What are you talking about? Were you spying on me? Like from the woods? Because I hardly even *spoke* to you until the night of the party at your mom's. My plants had been missing for weeks by then. Why would your mom have thought she could fix us up? According to you, I was a *suspect* or something." It made no sense.

There was a weird look on Lance's face—part reluctance, part pleading, part shame, part... doggy eyes? "I...." He sighed. "She's.... Lily gets ideas and...." He sighed again.

And that was that. Apparently, that was all Lance had to say. Tim felt a wave of bitter disappointment. God damn it all to hell, he hadn't even admitted to himself how much he hoped Lance would be able to talk him around. Stupid, stupid. Instead, all he'd really learned was that even their date night had been a joke, and that Lance couldn't lie worth shit. When would Tim ever learn? Anger and pain coursed through him.

He stood up abruptly. "I want you to leave."

"Tim, please," Lance begged. His nose twitched.

"Nope. I mean it. You have to go. *Now.*"

Lance closed his eyes as if the words were a blow. His face squinched up.

Maybe it was Lance's reaction—grief rather than anger—that gave Tim the courage to be firm. He grasped Lance's arm and tugged him to his feet, started marching him toward the door. He wasn't going to be a doormat anymore!

"Tim! I did like you! Even early on, and Lily knew it! She—"

"Out!"

"I know I'm not—" Lance's voice broke. He panted. "*huff*—explaining this well, but if you just—"

They reached the front door. Tim yanked it open, not looking at Lance, and tried to push him out. It didn't work. When Tim tugged on Lance's arm this time, Lance felt like a hundred eighty pounds of iron bar. Confused, Tim looked at his face.

247

Lance's mouth was slightly open, and he was panting hard. His eyes were wide with surprise, and he was rigid.

"Out?" Tim meant it as a command, but it turned uncertain in his mouth.

"Please! I j-j-just... ARROOOOOOO!" Lance threw back his head and made this noise. *What the ever loving hell?* It sounded exactly like a dog's howl. A finger of ice shot up Tim's spine, and his knees went weak. His anger evaporated in pure fear.

"L-lance?"

"AR-AR-AR-AROOOO!!!" Lance's head remained back, his body rigid. His fists were white-knuckle clenched at his side as if he were fighting something hard. The cry made Tim feel sick. It was the most mournful thing he'd ever heard. It was the sound of utter heartbreak. Before his eyes, Lance's hair seemed suddenly thicker, longer, and his day's stubble darkened rapidly, like time lapse photography.

Tim took a step back, his tongue frozen. What the fuck?

Lance panted and slowly forced his chin lower. His eyes were dazed, panicked. "S-sorrrrry. I—" *pant, pant,* "There's something I have to tell... C-chance. *He*-eeeeeeeeEEEEEE!"

Lance's words turned into a sad and painful whine and, from the look on Lance's face, it scared the crap out of him.

Lance jerked as if trying to head out into the night, but he didn't get more than a single step before he went rigid again. With another whine, he turned and ran back into the house. A moment later, Tim jumped when the bathroom door slammed shut.

*   *   *

Lance stared at the bathroom mirror and struggled against his dog nature, which was doing things to his body that had never happened before.

Lance was in pain and so was his dog. His dog thought Tim meant it. He was being cast aside, shut out in the cold. And his dog was refusing to go, refusing to leave his mate's side. Lance knew all of that, but he was still shocked as hell that his dog would come out against Lance's conscious will. He'd shifted that one time in his sleep, and that was bad enough, but he was fully conscious now.

He braced his palms against the sink's counter, breathing hard, trying to get a grip. He heard the back of his shirt rip and had an unbearable urge to fall to all fours.

No!

It wasn't so much that he wanted to hide this. In the back of his mind, he'd always thought he would eventually have to tell Tim the truth, show him. But not like this. Not while Tim was angry. Not without first *explaining,* preparing Tim. This would be like screaming "Watch out for the falling rocks!" after your friend was already flattened.

Except he wouldn't even be able to warn Tim then, would he? Because, oh yeah, he'd be a dog.

Tim pounded on the door. "Lance? What's going on? Should I call someone?" He sounded scared.

Lance didn't want Tim to be scared when he learned about the dog. This was happening all wrong. He looked into the eyes in the mirror and saw Chance's eyes. Tim thought they looked the same, but they really didn't. Chance's eyes were guileless and loving. Lance felt his heart growing in his chest, bursting through the human barriers and scars Lance carried. Chance's heart had none of that.

Maybe his dog did know best. Maybe he'd been right long ago, that Lance Beaufort would only fuck things up, had no idea

250

what to say or do. Chance had been the one who'd bonded with Tim in the first place. Maybe he should give himself over to pure instinct once again and trust Chance.

The bones in his shoulders and spine suddenly popped loudly as they broke, moved, shifted in a rush. It was as if his body had only been holding back waiting for that slight turn in Lance's will. He opened his belt with hands already growing hairy, his thumb shrinking. He had to get out of these clothes before undressing himself became impossible.

"Lance!" Tim shouted, afraid. He must have heard the popping bones.

Don't be afraid, Love. God damn it.

Lance struggled to find his words, even as he tore off his clothes. One last shot at this. "I'm... *I am Chance*. I b-b-became Chance to s-s-see what you were.... AR!" his fingers popped in agonizing fury, drawing in, his nails growing thick and long. He panted, struggling to finish, his voice a growl. "Didn't mean... harm, only see... Chance... fell in love with you. *I fell in love with you*—ooooo000OOO!"

And his words were gone.

*   *   *

I fell in love with you.

Tim couldn't believe what he'd heard. *I am Chance. I fell in love with you.* His brain couldn't even scoff at the words, or get purchase on its well-hewn skepticism, because there were those other sounds.

The sounds of bones breaking. Growls. A pained whine.

Lance. Holy hell, Lance is Chance. He's changing right now. He's in pain.

There was the sound of panting, a dog's stressed panting, and a quick series of those cracks.

"L-lance?"

Tim was in shock. His heart pounded, and his hands were damp. He put a hand on the doorknob, but he didn't dare open it.

This was insane. But the craziest part was... it wasn't that crazy. Was it? There were too many strange things that fell into place, like a rain of thudding frogs out of a clear blue sky. The way Chance had been so intelligent, the way he'd resisted playing doggy games at first, refused dog food. The way he'd

252

tried to hold himself aloof, wouldn't sleep in Tim's bed those first few weeks and had vanished every morning. *Of course he did. Lance works during the day.*

Then there were Chance's blue eyes, eyes exactly the same color as Lance's eyes, and those of everyone in his family. That thick, dark hair. Dear God, the birthmark on his ear *just where Chance had a spot.* The tuft of white on his black chest hair. His strange, starey intensity. And Lily! For the first time, her initial visit, her weird interest in him, and in hearing about Chance, made sense.

And Chance had disappeared for good the night Tim had spent time with Lance at the party. Lance had been so sympathetic about Chance's disappearance, and Lily so angry about it. Lance had brought him a puppy, almost appearing guilty about Chance being gone.

Dear lord, this can't be real. But the denial sounded fake even in his own head. He'd known Chance was special, hadn't he? Because he *was.* And Lance was special too, wasn't he? Tim thought about the earnest promises Lance had made in the car and at the restaurant, the way he didn't seem to have the filters or the shallow interest in sex normal guys had. Part of Tim was screaming, *Of course he's Chance! It makes so much* sense.

Tim listened hard, wanting more physical evidence that he wasn't crazy. There was silence from the bathroom. Then a whimpered cry of pain, a soft thud on the floor. Oh, God.

"Stop." He put his forehead on the door, shaky all over. "You don't have to do this. *Please*. If it hurts you. Please stop."

There was no sound except for the almost-not-there panting for a long moment as Tim strained to hear. Then came the sound of something shifting about. There was a scratch on the door, a dog's scratch. A soft, eager bark.

Chance's bark.

Tim closed his eyes against his now blurry vision. His stomach swam, his knees buckled, and something hot filled up his heart. Only the door held him up. There was another soft scratch on the other side. Filled with terror and longing and hope and dread, Tim turned the knob and opened it.

Lance's clothes were strewn about the bathroom floor. The tiny window in the shower was still closed. And sitting on the floor, looking healthy but wary, was Chance—big, beautiful Chance with his thick black fur and blue eyes. Those eyes watched him and waited. Intelligent. Loving. Sad. Resigned.

Tim wiped at his own eyes. "This is utterly fucking insane,

you know that?" he said, in a very wet voice.

Chance barked once. *Agreed.*

Tim fell to his knees and held out his arms, and Chance was there.

~15~

A Merry Chase

"WHY CAN'T I have you like this *and* have Chance at the same time?" Tim complained.

They were lying on the couch together, the way Tim had done with Chance. But Lance had shifted back and they were both human now, legs entwined and Lance back in the clothes he'd worn earlier.

"Um... because it doesn't work like that? Just like you can't be in here lazing on the sofa with me and in the kitchen making popcorn at the same time. More's the pity." Lance had grown very fond of the popcorn.

Tim huffed. "I don't see why not. There's already enough pixie dust in this whole deal to float an armada."

Lance inwardly rolled his eyes. "Well, I can't be both at once."

"Because I miss Chance. You have the best fur in the entire world. But I want you like this too."

"Life sucks," Lance said seriously. But honestly, he meant just the opposite. Life was *wonderful*. Inside he was bubbling with so much joy he felt like *he* could float right now. Pixie dust indeed.

He'd never really believed Tim could accept the truth. Sure, there were other quickened in the community that had bonded with, and married, humans, and those humans had accepted the secret and kept it. But Lance'd had little hope Tim would, not after the monumental mess he'd made of things.

"There are certain advantages to me being in this form, though." Lance rolled to pin Tim down and buried his nose in his neck, deeply inhaling his rich, earthy scent. Heaven.

Tim wriggled as if Lance's stubble tickled, but he didn't pull away. He wrapped his arms around Lance's neck and wriggled so he was on his back on the sofa and Lance was more fully over him. He held Lance's neck with those long, strong fingers of his as Lance nuzzled and licked his neck.

Suddenly, he pushed Lance away, his face curious. "Does it hurt when you do that? When you change? It sounded like it hurt."

Lanced sighed. "Yes. But you sort of… black out for the worst of it, like you fade out and fade back in."

"That sounds scary." Tim frowned.

"It is at first. Honestly, I don't change form often. Didn't for years once I started working. But most of the pack get together once a month for a 'howl at the moon' night where they change and run together or play. Most quickened believe it keeps them young."

"Quickened? Is that what you call it? How does it work exactly? I mean, can all dogs do it? Is this like a global dog conspiracy?"

Lance understood Tim had a thousand questions. He just wished they could go over them later. Because right then the scare of almost losing Tim had him needy for touch and scent. He was dying to bury his nose everywhere, to reassure himself Tim was there and was his. He wanted touch, not talk. But Lance forced himself to give a real answer.

"No, very few dogs can change. Honestly, we don't know the science behind it. There's a guy, Jason, who grew up in Mad Creek and got a PhD in genetics. He's off working in some lab somewhere trying to figure it out. What we do know is that a dog, an ordinary dog, can become quickened. We call that

258

'getting the spark'. It happens when a dog forms a very close bond with a specific human. Eventually, over a long period of time, that bond can trigger something in the dog that enables them to change form, to sort of... evolve to the next level."

Tim shifted as if getting more comfortable, his face intent. "Go on."

"Once that's happened, that dog's descendants are usually born quickened. My family has been in this area for three generations. Originally there was a human family, the Moffers, that owned a lot of this land and grew sheep."

"I've seen the name around town."

"Yeah, they're still here. Anyway, they also raised sheep dogs, border collies. And the family and the dogs became very codependent and tight. Generations of dogs and men completely bonded, living side by side 24/7. My great-great-grandfather was the first of the collies to become quickened, and two of his brothers did too. I was born this way. My mother and father were also born already quickened."

Tim narrowed his eyes thoughtfully. He smiled. "This is the coolest fucking thing in the world. Are there werewolves too? Vampires?"

Lance rolled his eyes. "Well, no vampires that I'm aware of. As for werewolves, that's a myth. Wolves are wild. They don't need or want to be anything except what they are. As far as I know, dogs are the only animal that can get the spark. I think it has to do with dogs being bred for thousands of years to be attuned to humans, living with them. But as I said, we don't really understand the science. I just try to deal with the reality."

"Reality!" Tim laughed sharply, as if that was the funniest thing.

Lance kissed him to shut him up. It was just getting loose and heated when Tim giggled into the kiss and broke it off.

"I guess I did look pretty suspicious."

Lance huffed. "You acted very nervous the first few times I met you."

"I have an eensy weensy problem with male authority figures."

"I never would have guessed that."

"And you were all intense and starey and—oh, shit! I totally see it now! Bordie collie! They're the ones that herd sheep, right?"

Lance sighed, giving up on instant gratification. He rolled

onto his side and played with that lank of floppy brown hair that always fell into Tim's face. He loved that lank of hair. "This is going to be weird for you for a while. There are other human pack members you can talk to. Bill McGurver, in fact. The vet? He's married to Jane McGurver, a quickened. He didn't know we existed either until he and Jane fell in love. So he can tell you what to expect."

Tim stared at him, eyes wide. "Do dogs, like, mate for life or something?"

"Quickened," Lance corrected. "Most quickened do mate for life, yes. Once we bond, it's almost impossible to lose that bond. We're very, very loyal."

"So… even if I do stupid things, or I'm a huge failure, or gain a thousand pounds or something… you'd still want me?"

Lance's nostrils flared, and he fought not to growl. Tim's insecurity bled not only into his carefully casual words, but also into every line of his body. Lance loathed the idea of anyone making Tim feel unworthy. He wanted to erase that, to see Tim confident in his own just-rightness. Maybe, in time, he could.

"Never. I will never stop loving you," he said firmly.

Tim's excitement melted into something softer, and he

threw an arm and a leg over Lance and stared at him. "I fell in love with you too," he said quietly. "I mean, I loved Chance so much, his soul. And the fact that Chance is *you*, that's like… like you couldn't even make up something that good."

"I'm glad you feel that way." Lance's voice was rough.

Tim appeared deep in thought for a while, his fists clenched in Lance's shirt. "You know what's weird? You told me in the car that one day I'd trust you. Well, through this whole thing, you never got angry with me. Even the night of the shooting, you were angry, but it wasn't at me. Even when I threw you out and wouldn't talk to you, you never threated me. You never even came close to raising a hand to me. You were just sad."

That broke Lance's heart. "Oh, Tim. I told you I'd never want to hurt you, no matter what you do."

"I… believe you?" Tim said, looking surprised. "I do. I believe you. Honestly, I trust you way more knowing you're Chance. It's like—like everyone has to have something hidden inside them, you know? And I'm afraid it's something nasty, like my dad had this really nasty thing inside him. So I tend to keep people at a distance. But now I know what's hidden inside you, and it's not something scary, it's the best thing in the world."

Lance was so grateful that he had no words. So instead he kissed Tim again. This time Tim kissed him back with enthusiasm, wrapping around him like the offspring of cling film and an octopus, and nearly sending them both sliding off the couch. Lance saved them by bracing a hand on the floor.

"So we can fool around now, right?" Tim asked. He leaned toward the floor teasingly, trying to get them to fall.

"You're going to break something," Lance growled. "Maybe we could move this to the bedroom."

"Is that an order, Officer?" Tim waggled his eyebrows suggestively.

"*Yes*," Lance growled, picking up his cue. Inside, Chance perked up his ears playfully. "On the bed. Naked. Now!"

Tim gave a delighted laugh, jumped up, and ran off to obey. And Lance, of course, had to give chase.

*　　　　　*　　　　　*

Tim tossed clothes as he went, hoping they'd distract Lance, and they did. He stopped and picked up each one, holding it to his nose, his eyes locked on Tim. The dark sparkle in those eyes—sky blue going almost navy with desire—promised things Tim sincerely hoped Lance meant to deliver.

The more aggressive Lance became, the giddier Tim felt, arousal and laughter building like an internal scream he could barely contain. Tim realized he really *did* trust Lance. Even though he'd just said it, words were only words after all. The feeling of security he had now as Lance stalked him, the freedom to express his desire without fear—that was real.

Tim stripped off his last article of clothing—his underwear. He had a moment of amazement at how hard he was just from the way Lance was looking at him.

Lance slowly moved closer, and Tim backed up against his bedroom wall.

"Okay, yeah," he managed, unable to keep it bottled up anymore. "I surrender. With no shots fired. Just—"

Lance took the last few steps fast and bent at the waist. For a moment, Tim had a weird idea Lance was going to head butt him. But instead, he grabbed Tim around the hips and tossed him over his shoulder.

Jesus, he was strong. Tim wasn't heavy, but he was taller

than Lance. Lance didn't just throw him onto the bed either. He stood holding Tim over his shoulder and buried his face into Tim's hip, snuffling and breathing him in.

"Oh, fuck." Tim braced his hand on Lance's upper back and tried not to wriggle as Lance's nose and tongue danced over his stomach. It should have been ticklish, but instead it was hot as hell. His erection was jammed against Lance's chest. And then, snuffling farther in toward ground zero, Lance tilted Tim's hips back until he could get his face at the junction of groin and thigh. Tim gave a tiny scream and grabbed the back of Lance's hips with both hands, afraid to fall, but Lance had his thighs in a firm hold. He held Tim easily, his nose buried in Tim's groin as if it was the best place on earth. Tim's erection brushed hopefully against Lance's cheek.

"Oh, Christ," Tim gasped, closing his eyes tight. This was like that Spiderman scene, only way better. Who knew being nuzzled and licked and smelled while basically hanging upside down over a guy's back could be so fucking hot? It was Lance's strength, the voracious, shameless interest in Tim's essence, the way he was doing whatever he wanted and all Tim could do was hang on for the ride.

But fuck, it felt like Lance could hang out there sniffing all day, and Tim really wanted more.

"Lance," he pleaded.

It seemed to get through, because Lance tossed Tim onto the bed. Tim reached up for him, but Lance stayed braced over Tim on his arms.

"Okay?" Lance asked. His eyes were stormy with lust, but Tim could sense that if he said it was too much, or seemed uncomfortable, Lance would turn sweet and gentle. And fuck that.

"More," Tim said. "More of everything. Except your clothes. Less of those."

Lance hurried to comply, standing to strip his shirt over his head and toss it. He kicked off his shoes and wrangled off his pants, underwear and socks in one go.

He stood fully naked before Tim for the first time. His body was all tight muscle. You could see his quads and biceps clearly, and he had those enticing V-shaped muscles from hips to groin that only Greek statues and male super models had. His chest hair was thick and black except for that lovely spot of pure white, and a trail ran down to an impressively thick and aroused cock. *Thank you, God.*

"Damn," Tim breathed.

Lance smirked, and he dove back in, running his nose and tongue over Tim's chest and then into—Christ!—his armpit.

Tim had always felt self-conscious about his body. He was a little on the skinny side, and he'd never lifted weights or anything. But Lance gave an excited whine in the back of his throat and seemed to gorge on nuzzling and scenting Tim, as if he was the best thing on earth. When Tim laughed at the tickling, and pushed Lance back from his armpit, Lance went for his groin again, sinking his nose deep into the area behind his balls, his tongue feasting on the fragrant space.

"Oh God," Tim gasped, more turned on than was probably healthy. Lance ran his nose and tongue up over Tim's balls and then up his shaft before sucking him inside with gusto and drawing on him in a way that made Tim's toes curl and his hands clench at Lance's shoulders. It was amazing, and worthy of at least a few years of intense study down the road, but right then Tim didn't want to come like that.

"Will you—will you fuck me and bite me in the neck? And will that mean we're mated forever?" Tim asked. It sounded like begging, but he didn't much care.

Lance laughed and raised his head. "We don't do that."

267

"Oh." That was disappointing.

Lance cocked his head and studied Tim's face for a moment. "Unless you... want me to?"

God, yes. "Only if you want to."

Lance got an evil little smirk. "Yeah? You mean you want me... here?" He canted Tim's hips up with two strong hands on the backs of his thighs and nosed deep into his crack. Tim felt a tongue lap delicately and then not so delicately over his rim. There was the gentle scrape of teeth.

"Shit!" He grabbed for the sheets. The world was tilting on its axis, and in a minute, he'd be on the ceiling. That probably meant death and destruction for mankind, but as long as this sensation continued, Tim was okay with that.

"That where you want me, baby?" Lance cooed, raising his head to fix Tim with blue eyes that were now shot through with a hurricane.

"*Yes,*" Tim gasped. "Right fucking there." And he did.

He'd only bottomed once before, with a guy who'd been as tentative as Tim himself. Despite the lack of chemistry, it had been an interesting sensation. They'd overkilled the prep, and there'd been no pain. Tim had liked the sensation of being filled.

He loved having his prostate stimulated as he jerked off, which is how that encounter had ended. He'd purchased a slender vibrator after that, which he used when he had a lot of time and was excessively horny. But this would be different. This would be more like the fantasies he had of being held down and fucked by a real man. Not cruelly, but covering him with confidence and assurance, like a big blanket that kept him safe and also, conveniently, unlike all but the most cleverly manufactured blankets, stimulated his prostate. Now that he was with Lance, it seemed like those fantasies had been a prophetic longing for him, specifically.

"I want you," Tim reiterated, in case it wasn't clear.

"Mmm." Lance moaned agreeably and went back to upending the universe with his tongue, adding a finger to the mix. *That* was a sensation Tim had never felt before, and because assurance was Lance's middle name—or maybe it was tenacity—Lance Assurance Tenacity Beaufort—it was like being rimmed by a gopher determined to burrow. And that was way hotter than it sounded.

"Oh my God," Tim said a few million times as Lance licked and gently worried with his teeth and fingers, completely devoted, as if he could do this forever.

269

"I'm ready now," Tim gasped, needing cock immediately. When Lance didn't relent, Tim half sat up to get into the bedside table drawer and pulled out a jar of lube and a condom. He scooped some lube onto two fingers and pushed Lance aside with his feet so he could plunge them where he needed them while Lance wrestled with the little foil packet.

"That's... interesting," Lance panted. By the intent look on his face as he stared at Tim's buried fingers, and absently rolled the condom on, what he meant was, 'That's gravy-covered prime rib and truffles'. Tim pulled his fingers out. "Now you." He grasped Lance's cock for the first time and slicked up the rubber.

This is it, this is the cock I will have for the rest of my life, Tim thought in a moment of clarity. Of all the cocks in the world, Tim thought he'd seriously lucked out getting this one, because it was plump and meaty without being freakishly huge. It still had all the original packaging intact, which Tim *loved*, and it was slightly narrowed at the tip and thick at the base. Made to the purpose, as it were.

"I love your cock," Tim said without meaning to. "And I really want to suck it, but I just put lube and, you know, *me*, all over it."

"Soon," Lance growled. "Fortunately, I can suck yours

270

now."

He was looking at Tim's cock again where it was snapped like an iron bar to his stomach. Lance started to dive for it, but Tim held him off by bracing two strong arms on his chest. "We should save that for later."

"Why?"

Lance was so genuinely perplexed, Tim laughed. "Because we have a lot of bedtime ahead of us to fill. Are you the kid who opened all his presents in the first five minutes on Christmas morning?"

"We'd be finding bits of paper for months," Lance agreed solemnly.

"I can imagine. Well, right now I want you here." Tim scooted down the bed a little and shifted his hips up, making the destination clear, all while holding and stroking Lance with one hand.

Lance was braced above Tim on his arms, and he made a funny sound at the touch of Tim's long-fingered hand. He closed his eyes, as if savoring it. So Tim stroked him with what he hoped was finesse, rubbing Lance's frenulum through the condom and sliding his foreskin over and off the plump head.

Lance's eyes squeezed tighter shut, and his hips started moving a little, his breathing growing ragged. Imagining what Lance was feeling, Tim's own cock pulsed in sympathy.

"Now, baby," Tim said. He didn't want to stop touching Lance, but he knew if he didn't, they'd never make it to penetration.

Lance opened his eyes, locked them on Tim's, heaved a deep breath in through his nostrils, and guided himself into place. Poised at the entrance, he placed his hands on the back of Tim's thighs once more, rolling him up so that Tim was more open and displayed than anyone with a teeny tiny crumb of modesty could feel comfortable with, and all Tim could think of was *now*.

Tim didn't trust his voice so he nodded. And Lance sank in.

Despite the fact that he was significantly larger than the device Tim was used to, he met with little resistance. He was sucked intractably inward as if Tim's body was absorbing him in a way much deeper than mere sexual penetration.

When he was sunk to the root, Lance ground against Tim, as if he could get deeper still. His intense blue eyes were fixed on Tim's face, and there was a sheen of delighted wonder over his entire aspect.

272

"You like this?" Lance asked him, as if he could hardly believe it.

Tim answered sincerely. "I love it."

"Me too."

"Then do it." What he really meant was *Take me like you mean it, take me like you own me.* And maybe Tim didn't have the balls to say it, but he didn't need to, because Lance seemed to read it on his face.

He pushed Tim's thighs in closer to his chest, forcing him almost past the point of comfort, and then he drew out and slammed back in, repeating the motion again and again while pinning Tim with the intensity of his gaze. One hand kept Tim canted upward while the other grabbed Tim's cock, not stroking it but loosely squeezing, so that the motion of their fucking shifted it in his fist in a delightfully filthy way.

Mine, Tim imagined Lance saying, and then, as the assault on the sensitive tissue of ass and cock grew into a triumvirate of *too much, oh god more,* and *I'm going to come,* he realized he was hearing the word for real. Lance was chanting it under his breath with every thrust, and growing louder.

"Mine. You are, aren't you?"

"Yes."

They were both so close. Tim felt the pleasure building to the point of no return, and he could feel the tremor in Lance's thrusts and in the clenched ecstasy on his face. In an instant, Tim pulled his thigh away from Lance's hand, put his feet on Lance's chest and pushed him back, forcing him to pop free. Ow.

Lance stared at him with surprise. "Those feet are dangerous."

"Wanna finish like this." Tim flipped onto his stomach and pushed himself up onto hands and knees. He was too far gone to feel self-conscious about his desire, and he wanted this, wanted Lance covering him with his hand tight around Tim's cock from behind.

Lance said nothing, but he took position fast, pushing back in with tormenting slowness, causing them both to groan at the intense sensation on their hypersensitized bits. He allowed Tim to pull his hand around, and fingers entwined, they both gripped Tim's painfully swollen cock.

"I need to come," Tim gasped.

"Got this," Lance gritted out, his voice tortured.

He slammed into Tim again and again, no finesse now, just

pure instinct. Tim tilted his hips just right to get Lance rubbing his prostate with every in and out. It was blindingly good and as intense as anything Tim had ever felt in his life. It was as intense with *good* and *pleasure* and *connection* as anything in his life had ever been bad, as if everything that had led up to now, no matter how shitty, had been worth it just for this moment here.

As he trembled on the brink, Tim remembered that he wanted this to be forever in a way that no one could take from him, so he raised his shoulders slowly, clasping Lance's other hand where it was fixed on his hip to show he didn't want to stop, and straightened until both of them were on their knees. He squeezed where he and Lance were stroking his cock and pushed back into Lance's chest, tilted his neck to the side to bare it.

Lance took the hint and closed his mouth over the tendon there, sucking hard and gently biting as he thrust. And that was how bliss found them as they both dove off the cliff together.

They lay on the bed like broken toys for a time, Tim on his stomach, smushing come into the sheets, and Lance on his back with both legs and one arm thrown over Tim's body.

"I need to find and burn all your Twilight books," Lance said at last.

"Team Jacob," Tim muttered, drooling onto his pillow a bit. He managed to raise a less than enthusiastic fist of solidarity. He didn't need to tell Lance he had never owned nor read a Twilight book. His little garage apartment had been rigged into Marshall's HBO.

"I suppose I should be grateful you were mentally prepared."

Tim snorted. "For you?" He turned his head on the pillow so he could take in the gorgeous, naked man in his bed. His cock looked succulent where it rested limp on his thigh. "Hate to break this to you, but nothing could have prepared me for you, big guy."

Lance's blue eyes were soft for once. He ran a slow finger down Tim's spine.

"Yeah? So are you Team Lance now?"

Tim just blinked sleepily at him. He wanted to say *I hope you meant all that bonding shit, because I won't give you back, ever.* But he figured that would sound needy. Besides, the way Lance was looking at him practically said the same thing.

Renfield scratched at the bedroom door and whined.

"There are two chicken dinners sitting in a brown bag on

276

your kitchen counter," Lance pointed out. "I think Renfield's tired of waiting for his share."

"Race ya!" Tim said, sitting up eagerly.

"I'm not *racing* you. I'm—"

But Tim was already out of bed. He flung open the bedroom door and ran for the kitchen, naked and laughing.

He could hear Lance's bare feet as they pounded after him and the sound of his laughing growl.

~16~
Attack

"STOP!" Tim yelled with horror as Lily trod right through his row of baby lettuces.

Lily stopped moving and looked down at where she was standing. The infant leaf of a ruby red lettuce peeked out from under her shoe like the Wicked Witch of the West after Dorothy's house fell on her. "Oh. Sorry! I saw a rabbit."

Tim marched down the aisle between the mounded rows and grabbed her elbow. "Out! You are hereby banished from the field. I mean it! Don't make me get you one of those invisible fence and collar thingys."

He steered her clear of the plants, marched her between the rows, and shoved her onto the grass beside the field.

"But I can help weed!" Lily complained.

"You pulled up all my radishes yesterday. No more

278

'weeding' for you!"

Gus chuckled. He was among the young green pea shoots fixing a frame made from PVC pipes and nylon mesh so the peas could climb. Unlike Lily, Gus seemed to really enjoy gardening work, and he was very diligent about following Tim's instructions. Tim had learned that Gus was a bulldog that had gotten 'the spark' and was new at this whole human thing. Even though Tim couldn't pay him right then, Gus wanted to learn and he was a sweet, agreeable guy to have around. Lily, on the other hand….

"Black thumb," Tim pointed at Lily. "Banished. Sorry."

"But I want to help!" Lily pouted. "I need to help you, Tim. I *owe* you, and you're practically my son-in-law! That's what families do!"

Tim still hadn't completely forgiven Lily for stealing his seed trays. But at the mention of family, Tim went a little gooey in the center.

"Okay. What about this. Can you make up a few buckets of compost tea in the greenhouse? And then maybe you can help with dinner. Lance said he'd be done with work early tonight so he should be here any minute."

"Fine," Lily sniffed. Then her eyes narrowed and darted around the grass. "Rabbit!" And she was off. Renfield had been panting in the shade of a nearby tree, but he bounded after her as if it was a game.

Tim took off his gardening gloves and stuffed them into the belt he wore with his assorted plant markers, twine, and tools. He stood and looked over the field.

The plants he'd managed to salvage were all in the field now along with rows of lettuces, peas, and green beans, all planted directly into the ground. There was still a lot of empty space, but it was room to grow. He went to check on the roses.

Tim had planted the traumatized rose seedlings that had escaped 'the night of the broken glass' in a plot in front of the cabin, making Linda a little rose garden. Of the hundred or so rose hip seeds he'd lovingly set to germinate, only twenty now lived, and he had no idea what was what since all of his markers had been thrown about and misplaced that night. About half the plants had at least one small bud. He'd give them more compost tea today and keep his fingers crossed. It was a little like opening an unmarked treasure box. Odds were low he'd get the lavender-tipped cream Linda was looking for, but he hoped there'd be something nice enough to assuage her and his own sense of responsibility for the rent.

Lance's cruiser pulled up in the driveway. Tim straightened and smiled. It had only been two weeks since they'd gotten together for real, but it felt like a lifetime. Or rather, it felt like a lifetime about to be lived, like a huge boulder poised to roll down a hill—unstoppable and terrain-altering.

"Hey." Lance approached him wearing those mirrored shades, a day's stubble, and a serious glower. But when he reached Tim, he wrapped his arms around Tim's waist and lifted him off the ground, swinging him around.

"Show off," Tim snorted, despite his huge, world-eating grin.

"Mmmm. Mine." Lance nuzzled Tim's neck and gave it a play bite. He still teased Tim about the werewolf stuff, but Tim knew he secretly liked it as much as Tim did.

"I asked Lily to make dinner, but she chased off a rabbit instead. She may not be back before dark."

"If we're lucky. Maybe the rabbit's migrating through. Maybe she'll chase it all the way to Alaska."

"A Canadian snow rabbit? We can only hope."

Lance put Tim down and backed up, his face stony again.

"What is it?"

Lance took off his glasses and tucked them away. His eyes avoided Tim's gaze. "I have to work tonight. The DEA is doing a sting on that cannabis farm in Coarsegold, and they asked me to be on-site. They're hoping to identify the men who shot this place up."

"But you never saw the men," Tim said, his heart rate ratcheting up instantly. *And I don't want you anywhere near that.*

"Roman saw them. He's going to be there too, and I should be with him. Besides, this is my sting since I reported it."

Tim knew Lance had been working with the DEA since the night of the shooting. But he hadn't expected it to boil down to direct confrontation.

Lance must have read his fear, because he put a hand on Tim's shoulder. "There's nothing for you to worry about. The DEA will have SWAT there to secure the place. I won't be in the fire fight."

"But you could be. You'll have your gun, and you'll be right there. I know you. If you sense an opening, or that someone is hurt, you'll run right into it—like Lily goes after rabbits."

Lance smiled. "I promise, I won't go after the drug dealers the way Lily goes after rabbits."

"You'd better not! Because if you get hurt or shot or, god forbid, killed, I will be seriously pissed off." Tim barely refrained from stamping his foot. He knew he was being childish, but he didn't care.

Lance rubbed Tim's shoulder with a sad smile. "It's my job. You'll have to get used to being attached to an officer of the law."

Tim was still not happy, but his sense of humor sparked at the word. "Attached? Is that like there's an invisible thread going from here." Tim put his hand on his heart. "To here," he touched Lance's breastbone, his eyes wide and purposefully dewy. "And if we got too far apart it would snap and I would commence to bleed inwardly?"

Lance rolled his eyes. "God help me. Now it's Jane Eyre."

"Aha! How do you know it's Jane Eyre?"

Lance's face went a little pink. "Lily has watched every movie version of Jane Eyre ever created. Repeatedly."

"And she *forced* you to watch with her. I see."

Lance stiffened his back, his chin raising a little. "It

couldn't be avoided. I have excellent hearing."

God, Lance was so adorable when he had that guilty-defensive thing going on. And suddenly, thinking about the fact that Lance was walking into danger tonight, made Tim crave him desperately. His body went from amusement to *touch me* from one heartbeat to the next.

"How much time do you have before you have to leave?" he asked, his voice dropping an octave.

Lance perked up. His nostrils flared as he sniffed the air. There was a low whine in his throat, and he pulled Tim in by his hips and pressed against him. "Long enough."

*   *   *

"Sheriff, Mr. Charsguard, you two stay put. Once we have the suspects in custody, we'll ask for your help identifying them. Clear?"

The DEA special agent in charge, Harrison, was an older man with cropped gray hair, but he radiated authority. Lance was more than happy to give him the lead.

"Clear," Lance answered.

"Yes, sir," Roman said after a moment's hesitation, as if unsure if he should speak or not.

"Good." Harrison nodded and moved away, his eyes and his mind on the SWAT team that was arrayed in the darkness around the house in the woods. They'd been quiet getting into place, but Lance had a feeling the men inside the house knew something was up. The lights in the front room had gone out a minute ago. The suspects were either going to try to escape— though they had to know the back of the house was covered—or they were behind those dark windows with guns, ready to fight. Lance hoped they weren't stupid enough to fight. Surely they knew they couldn't win?

He and Roman stood behind the SWAT team near an armored van. Beside him, Roman was stiff and tense. Lance understood. The dog inside Lance was hyped up and anxious, metaphorically pacing back and forth. It had to be far worse for Roman, whose human instincts were so nascent.

Lance put a hand on his arm in silent command. *Hold.*

Two dark figures in SWAT uniforms detached themselves from the shadows and ran in a crouch for the front door. Three things happened almost simultaneously. One of the men's faces was illuminated in the moonlight as he turned his head to his

285

partner—under his helmet he was young, square-jawed, and stubbled. Gunfire erupted from the front windows of the house, shattering the glass. And Roman Charsguard pulled away from Lance's hand and ran straight into enemy fire.

Lance froze. The immediate imperative was strong. *Pack. Aid. Protect.* Roman was Lance's responsibility. He couldn't let a member of his pack drown alone.

But the human side of him spoke up: *Tim.* He'd promised Tim he wouldn't do anything rash, that he'd stay out of it tonight. And he wanted to fulfill his promises to Tim—including the ones he hadn't yet made, the ones that were stored in his bones. He wanted to give Tim a good life, to keep him safe, to be there to ensure he was well and happy. Lance wanted that with everything he was.

This was why he'd decided not to mate, wasn't it? Because he'd believed there was no way to divide his loyalty, to be true to both his pack and his mate and children. If Lance was lucky, he'd be like his own father, dying relatively young from a heart attack, having worked himself to death. And if he was not lucky, he'd die like this. He should never have started things with Tim. It wasn't fair.

And then, in a moment of clarity, he saw that it wasn't

either/or. Tim loved Lance for who he was, and that included the way he protected his pack. Having Tim as a mate didn't mean he couldn't do his job. It just meant he had to be smart as hell about it, and do whatever he could to not leave Tim a widower. But if that happened.... Well. At least they would have had every second possible together. It was worth it.

With new resolve, Lance assessed the situation, his eyes darting round the scene. The two SWAT men that had been going for the front door were down on the ground on their bellies, getting as flat as possible, too far from cover to move. Harrison was yelling orders and the SWAT team opened fire on the house, trying to give their men cover. And Roman—he was crouched so impossibly low to the ground he almost looked like a spider as he crawled forward fast. He hadn't shifted, but Lance could see the German shepherd in every line of his body. It was beautiful and brave and so incredibly dangerous.

Lance darted forward, crouching down, though not able to get nearly as low as Roman. The SWAT team was still firing so heavily that it didn't seem like anything was coming from the house. But there were bullets in the air, and the chances of being hit by friendly fire was enormous.

He dimly heard Harrison screaming at him to get back.

Then he reached Roman. Who was about to get his head blown off.

Roman and the young officer he'd gone after were on the ground. The SWAT guy had rolled onto his side. Roman, had his hands on the man's upper arms and the SWAT guy had his gun in his hand, pointed right at Roman's face. They stared at one another.

Jesus fucking Christ.

The policeman was young, but he didn't look scared. He did, thankfully, hesitate in pulling the trigger. Perhaps it was the look on Roman's face. Lance knew immediately what the young SWAT officer must think. Roman wasn't in a uniform, he was in camouflage pants and a brown canvas jacket. He was big and threatening, dark-haired and intense. But on his face was a look that was… fuck. It was disappointment. Resignation. Grief.

Roman wanted the man to pull the trigger, Lance realized with a sense of horror.

"Stand down!" He shouted over the gunfire. "He's with us! Stand down!"

The young SWAT officer darted his eyes at Lance, taking in his sheriff's uniform. He didn't lower the gun, but he did look less ready to pull the trigger.

"He's a civilian, a witness. He's unarmed. Stand down!"

The SWAT officer swallowed, visibly, and lowered the gun. Roman's face went blank.

"Roman, draw back!" Lance ordered.

The gunfire stopped abruptly. In the background, Harrison was barking orders. Lance knew the SWAT fire had stopped because of them, because they were in the way, but that meant the men in the house would be returning fire any second now.

He grabbed Roman's arm, but Roman pulled away. That's when Lance saw the blood. The young SWAT officer's left arm trembled, bloodied, on the ground. He'd been shot.

"Get you safe," Roman muttered to the man. Ignoring the fact that there was still a gun in the man's right hand, Roman moved around him, put his hands under the officer's shoulders, and began dragging him toward the SWAT line. The man didn't fight him but went limp, probably weak from loss of blood.

It was the longest damn five seconds of Lance's life. He drew his gun and covered Roman and the injured officer as Roman dragged the dead weight through the browned grass. Lance stood between them and the house, facing those shot out windows, gun raised, stepped backward as quickly as Roman was moving. The house was like a waiting bomb. Lance had no cover, and at any moment, a bullet could shatter his brain or his heart.

Tim. I love you. Tim.

They reached cover, SWAT men closing a line in front of them, and Lance went weak with relief. It was not his day to die then. Not today. There was gunfire from the back of the house and Harrison waved the team forward while simultaneously speaking into a walkie-talkie.

"In the rear! They're headed for the woods. Go!"

Lance and Roman stood near the ambulance. Lance's heart rate had finally returned somewhat to normal, though part of him was itching to go where the action was. The men who'd been in the house, about a dozen of them, had attempted to make a run for it during the distraction provided by Roman and Lance. The SWAT team was hunting them down now. Lance could hear them off in the distance. But, itch aside, he was content to stay with the ambulance and vans.

Roman was staring at the ambulance. The doors were open,

and they were trying to stabilize the young officer who'd been shot.

"I thought… I thought I saw James. But it wasn't him," Roman said at last.

Oh. Lance didn't know what to say. There was so much dull heartbreak in those words, and somehow lurking beneath Roman's stoic face, that Lance found it unbearable.

The human in him had no words, but his dog offered comfort in the only way it could. Lance pulled Roman into a hug and nuzzled at his short hair. He wanted to lick for comfort, but he was far enough away from his canine ancestors to refrain, even though he didn't mean it sexually and Roman was dog enough not take it that way. Lance just rubbed his nose in Roman's hair and stayed there, holding him tight. *Pack.*

Roman was stiff and cold initially, but he gradually relaxed, going soft in Lance's arms, his body heavy with grief.

"Why do we have to survive them?" It was a child's question, or that of an angry man who thought life was crueler than he himself would ever be.

"I don't know, Roman."

"I was something with him. I had a purpose. I don't know

who I am like this."

The words were simple, but they came from Roman's heart. Lance could feel his stress and sadness. He could smell it.

Lance thought of Tim, and how everything had changed since Tim appeared. Strange. Even if you were sure you knew who you were—you could be completely wrong.

"You will. I promise you. It takes time. But you have a place with us. And work to do."

Roman pulled back. "I endangered us both tonight," he spat out. "You'd be right to want me as far from the sheriff's department as possible."

Lance knew this was a hard admission for him, a point of self-loathing from which he might never recover. Lance couldn't let that happen. He grabbed Roman's arms and yanked him back so Roman was meeting his eyes. Roman lowered his at once, submissive but still angry.

"You probably saved that man's life. And we wouldn't have found this base if it weren't for you."

"But I ran into live fire. I disobeyed the team leader. I could have made it all worse! I could have gotten you killed."

Roman was no dummy, and Lance couldn't really argue

with him. "Okay, that's true. But what would James say about a soldier who makes a mistake? I bet he'd say the man learns his lesson and carries on, becomes wiser and stronger. Wouldn't he? Are you a quitter, Roman?"

Roman's jaw firmed up, and his spine straightened. "No, sir."

"Good. Because I have the feeling this isn't the end of this battle. I need you."

Lance said it to encourage Roman, but even as he did, the words had a feeling of truth. Just because they'd taken down this one farm didn't mean there weren't others, or that this was over. And now the dealers knew about Mad Creek. It was a good place for secrets—remote, uncelebrated, off the beaten path. For the first time, his town's very anonymity felt dangerous. His pack wasn't the only one with secrets to hide.

"Hey!"

Lance let go of Roman, and they both turned. A medic was ready to close the ambulance door, but he waited as the officer who'd been shot struggled to raise himself on his good arm. With his helmet off, he looked even younger than before, his face pale with pain and grim.

"Thanks," the man called gruffly. He was looking right at Roman. Roman stared back. He nodded once in acknowledgment.

The medic shut the door, and the ambulance pulled away.

~17~

Howling at the Moon

IT WAS a fine, warm night in June when Tim and Lance pulled up to join the slew of cars at the picnic shelter in Foster Park. The park was halfway up Beacon Mountain, and Tim noticed on the way in that its entrance was purposefully unkempt. There were no hiking trails, benches, or trash cans in Foster Park, according to Lance. There was nothing that would appeal to outsiders. The large picnic shelter made of logs was tucked away in the back behind a cluster of trees.

Foster Park was where the pack had its Howl at the Moon night once a month during the full moon. Not, according to Lance, because the full moon had any particular power over them, but because it kept the nighttime woods from being dark as pitch.

Tim was bouncing with excitement as Lance grabbed the beer cooler from the back of his truck. Tim himself juggled a tray of crackers and his homemade pesto sauce—made with the first basil of the season—and Rennie's leash.

"This is awesome!" he said, as he picked out people he knew milling about the open log shelter. There were more surrounding a roaring campfire nearby.

And it *was* awesome. It was fucking mind-blowing being at a party night for *shifters*. How cool was that? Also, Tim was happy to see some of the people he'd come to care about—Gus, Daisy, Fred Beagle from the post office, and, yes, even Lily. At least she wouldn't be trampling over his plants tonight, and it was hard to pretend he didn't secretly like her mothering. At least he didn't mind it when she aimed it at his stomach or cabin rather than his plants or his love life.

But side-by-side with the awesomeness, there was a lingering apprehension and a pinprick of fear. This was the first time he was going to be around the pack when they were in their dog forms.

"You're sure no one's gonna shift in front of us mere mortals? I want to be mentally prepared." Tim asked Lance, for probably the hundredth time, as they walked toward the campfire.

"Nope. We go into the woods to change."

"Okay," Tim said doubtfully. "I hope so, because I remember the sounds of those breaking bones. And *seeing* it..." he shuddered. "I'd rather not end up screaming like a little horror movie girl and embarrassing you."

"Don't scream," Lance deadpanned. "That will make all the dogs attack you."

Tim huffed and glanced at Lance sideways, trying to read his face. "Ha ha. Very funny."

"Also, being licked to death is not a euphemism. Not here," Lance intoned menacingly.

Tim snorted, though his heart tripped a little faster. "Good thing I skipped my prime rib body wash then and used the peanut butter. Dogs don't like peanut butter, right?"

Lance dropped the cooler onto the grass, growled a laugh, and grabbed Tim around the waist.

"Pesto!" Tim gasped, as Lance leaned in and nuzzled him over the platter. He licked Tim's neck. "Very rare and very precious pesto! And I was, um, kidding about the peanut butter." Tim squirmed in ticklish pleasure.

"Yes, but what a brilliant idea," Lance breathed against his ear. "I can think of all *sorts* of places to put peanut butter. Or the pesto, if you prefer."

Tim laughed. The idea of his dick being covered in pesto was unexpectedly hilarious. *Wrong*, but still very funny.

"Oh, you two!" Lily pulled them apart like taffy and hugged Tim to her bosom.

"Pesto!" Tim said.

"I don't get first hug?" Lance sounded insulted.

Lily hugged him too. "You've gotten my hugs all your life. Tim needs them more. Besides, he convinced you to come tonight for the first time in, what, five years? He deserves a hug just for that."

Lance grunted in agreement.

"So who's minding the store tonight?" Lily asked.

"Charlie's at the station and Roman's watching the road to the park. I'm sure it'll be a quiet night, but they've both got Tim's cell number just in case."

"Where's the food table?" Tim asked, brandishing the platter. He wanted to put the endangered pesto on a flat surface as soon as possible.

"In the picnic shelter, pup!" Lily said happily. Lance said

298

she called everyone she considered young a 'pup'. It didn't seem to faze her that Tim had no dog in him. The endearment made Tim smile.

He headed for the shelter, cruelly leaving Lance to wrangle Lily and Renfield.

In the shelter, Tim placed his platter next to an array of other goodies and took the foil off the top.

"Hey, Tim." Bill McGurver smiled at him and extended a hand. "I was just scoping out the menu. Word to the wise: get in the front of the line. This crew will demolish every morsel on here in ten minutes flat."

"Good to know."

"What's that? Pesto?" Bill leaned forward to peer at the platter. Tim had arranged some crudités and crackers Lily had brought him around the bowl of green stuff.

"Yes. The veggies are store bought. Mine aren't ready yet. But the pesto was made with my own basil. Want to try?"

Bill looked intrigued, so Tim scooped some pesto onto a cracker and handed it to him. Bill took a bite and his eyes grew big.

"Oh, wow. That's amazing. I've never been a big fan of

pesto, but you just converted me. You really grew the basil yourself?"

Tim shrugged, but he was pleased at the reaction. "Basil's easy. It doesn't have any serious pest or disease issues. And it's best really fresh like this. I picked it this afternoon."

"Oh, man! If you decide you want to sell this stuff, I'll be first in line." Bill snuck another cracker and dipped it.

Tim considered it. "Next weekend will be my first time at the Mad Creek farmer's market. I'll have basil there, and I could do recipe cards?"

"Great! I'll be there. Jane would love this, and I've been doing more cooking since the baby arrived. Hey, I wanted to say… I'm really happy for you and Lance. *Really* happy."

Bill looked very sincere, and Tim found himself doing an 'aw shucks' thing with the toe of his Converse. He made himself stop. "Thanks."

"Lance has needed someone in his life for a long time. But he's always been so serious and work-driven. I guess it's in his collie nature to feel he has to be on guard all the time."

"I know, right? It so is!" It was a relief to be able to talk to someone like Bill McGurver, someone who knew Lance and also knew what Lance was under the surface. "You don't—you don't think it's wrong for me to distract him from that, do you?" Tim had wondered. He wanted Lance to be with him as much as possible, and to be focused on them when he was. But he realized Lance was important to the town, and sometimes he worried he was being horribly selfish.

"Not even a little bit." Bill smiled. "He's a better man for it already. Lance could always be... a little intense."

Tim snorted.

"In fact, that night I found him at your place, 'hit by your car', I was honestly worried he'd crossed the line into full-blown crazy cop territory."

"You could say that. But looking back, it is pretty funny. I mean, that you knew who he was that night and I had no clue."

Bill smirked. "Did you give him that bath I suggested?"

"Ooh, yeah!" Tim grinned, remembering it vividly. He should probably feel like an idiot, but the idea of uber-serious Lance being put through a shampooing was pretty hysetrical. "You want to hear how it went?"

"Every. Last. Detail."

Tim left Bill laughing so hard he had to just wave to say good-bye, tears streaming down his cheeks. Still chuckling, Tim joined Lance and Lily by the campfire. By some magic signal, the group headed for the food tables in the shelter. And, yes, Bill had been right. The food was sucked up like sand in a tornado. Fortunately, Tim was at the front of the line with Lance and Lily. By the time the meal was over, he'd gotten three more requests for his pesto recipe and promises to visit him at the farmer's market for the basil.

Not long after dinner, Tim noticed people slip away, usually with big smiles and a sense of excitement. Lily left first, Renfield padding along after her. Gus went next, practically skipping his way into the woods. Clearly, he couldn't wait to be a dog again. Janine, looking very sleek in black pants and a sweater, left with more casual grace but no less of a gleam in her eye. Lance's brothers and their wives escaped, leaving their kids in the nominal care of Mrs. Beagle, but actually just running around with shrieks and giggles.

Before long, there were only a dozen full-blooded humans sitting around the campfire. Them and Lance, who was still at Tim's side.

Tim nudged him. "Aren't you going to go play?"

Lance shrugged. "I'd rather keep an eye on things. Make sure everyone's safe. And stay with you."

Tim felt the spur of a challenge. He quirked an eyebrow. "You mean... I'll have to find some other canine to have fun with? Hmm. Maybe Janine would like to play ball."

Lance narrowed his eyes at Tim, unamused.

By then, dogs were appearing back into the clearing. Tim could hardly believe, looking at them, that they were all shifters, people he'd *met*. Like Lance, they looked like actual dogs, dogs of all shapes and sizes, purebreds and mutts. But there was something special about all of them, a kind of glow, and elevated aura that surrounded them. And the overall mood was joyous. Inwardly, Tim relaxed in places he hadn't known he was worried. This was more than okay. This was fucking magical. And also weirdly normal at the same time. He felt like the luckiest person on earth.

Lance's brothers and their mates came trotting out of the trees, and they played with their delighted kids in the grass beyond the campfire. Tim knew Lance's brothers on sight—all of them black collies with blue eyes. None of them were as special as Lance or as handsome. Then again, Tim was a little bit biased.

"Welp! I'm going to go run in the woods," he said decisively, standing up. "Don't worry about me. Stay here by the fire and relax. I probably won't trip over tree roots and break my neck. Or fall into a wasp's nest and get stung. Or find some furry companion to hug and pet. Out there in the dark."

Tim took off at a trot, barely suppressing his laughter. He heard Lance growl warningly behind him and knew he'd won.

Tim passed blurred shapes in the woods as he ran, crashing through the trees in the giddy joy of being chased. He heard distant happy barks and the still creepy, but no longer as ominous, sound of bones snapping in the dark.

The woods were dim, but the light of the full moon was bright enough for him to make out the path he was on. He was getting worried about how far he'd gone when he sensed a presence running up behind him. He turned to see Chance. His black fur was lost in the shadows but glints of moonlight struck through it like strands of silver and those brilliant blue eyes shone bright. His tongue was out and he looked like he was grinning.

Tim laughed out loud and kept running. Lance passed him so he could lead the way. They went several miles down a trail, winding farther away from the sounds of the group and heading up a steep path. Chance pulled ahead, and Tim lost sight of him. He continued up the trail anyway, calling Lance's name. The damn route must have been built by a mountain goat, because even Tim's long legs had to stretch to scramble up the final ascent.

When he pulled himself up into the open, he was on an outcropping at the top of a hill. There was a view of mountains on all sides and the valley below was dimly illuminated by the moon and stars, deep black shadows soft among the silvery blue. It was quiet except for the sound of someone breathing very hard. Tim turned to see Lance, human and naked, crouched a few feet away.

Tim drew in an involuntarily gasp. Lance looked wild like this—his bunched muscles sheened with sweat and dirt, his hair mussed, and something in the set of his mouth and eyes still very much animal.

Tim shuddered with a wave of lust. "Hey," he whispered.

Lance said nothing. He seemed to have one foot in the other world and no interest in leaving it. There was something dark and compelling in that. Especially when Lance moved closer, still crouched, and began nosing at Tim, trailing his mouth up one leg, smelling deeply, and then on up his side, slowly rising to his feet to follow the line of Tim's body.

Lance didn't reach for Tim's clothes, but he was erect and the scent of his desire was tangible in the air. It was thrilling. Tim unzipped his jacket and tossed it, then pulled his T-shirt over his head while Lance continued to lick and nuzzle him, under his arm, then in the curve of his neck, a low growl in his throat all the while.

"Oh, fuck, that's hot," Tim muttered while doing his best to unzip and discard his pants and underwear. He only just managed not to send them sailing over the side of the cliff and gave a hysterical little giggle at the idea of walking back into camp naked from the waist down.

Lance growled a little harder and latched onto Tim's neck, gently, with his teeth. Tim forgot all about laughing. "Oh. Oh, God."

With that light bite, Lance guided them both to the ground and then pulled and nuzzled and pushed til Tim was on all fours.

Tim had a few dregs of his logical brain still online, enough to wonder at himself, to be surprised at how hot this was. But it fucking *was*. Out there in the night, naked on a mountain top, with Lance's beautiful and very male human form, but the

306

beast still prowling just below the skin. There was something dangerous and primal about the animal nature—completely unself-conscious, focused, unashamed, and lost in its mate, driven by pure instinct.

And then Lance nuzzled between Tim's cheeks and began to lick him *there*. Tim's mind rolled over and joined Lance in letting chemistry rule.

Lance licked and worried at Tim, opening him up. He didn't use his fingers. His hands were braced on the ground, arms on either side of Tim's hips. And there was something incredibly sexy about that, about the single attention of his enthusiastic mouth, about being touched by nothing but the cool night air, the wafts of heat radiating off Lance's body behind him, and those lips, probing tongue, and teeth. Tim panted and moaned and tried to dig his fingers into the dirt beneath them.

"Lance, please," he begged at last. "I need you. Need you now."

Lance obliged. He rose onto his knees, laved Tim with spit, used his hand to gather pre-cum from Tim's cock and spread it on his own, added saliva, and then grabbed Tim's hips. He wasn't rough, but he was insistent, urgent. He penetrated Tim with one long, slow thrust.

Tim's head dropped onto his arms. "Fuck."

He spread his legs wider and canted his hips back, inviting his lover to take him. And Lance did. He held on to Tim's hips with both hands and pounded into him to the point of pain. A breeze ruffled Tim's hair and painted goose bumps down his spine, and the sharp bite of Lance's cock became a lustful thrill that curled Tim's toes. Lance was pounding him open—body and mind both, *owning* him, and Tim had never felt so high on arousal or so alive.

He shifted his hips slightly, so that Lance was hitting that sweet spot inside him, and bliss ramped up with every thrust.

"Can't—" Tim managed, feeling his testicles tighten and his cock throb where it hung heavily down between his legs. Christ, he was going to come untouched.

Lance made an incomprehensible sound above him and pounded even harder, his thighs shaking and his fingers gripping tight, his breath soft grunts. The sound and feel of his desperation was enough to send Tim flying. The first pulse hit the ground, and Tim grabbed himself with one hand and squeezed, so intensifying the sensation that a cry left his throat.

"*Lance!*"

Lance stiffed behind him, threw back his head, and let go. His howl rang out into the night, a vibration of life, a wild echo of ecstasy and joy.

~Epilogue~

BY AUGUST, Tim was used to the routine, but it was still grueling. In Santa Barbara, he'd worked hard, but he had peace and quiet in the greenhouse. Now at the head of his own produce business, he did everything. His crops were in their August abundance and needed regular weeding and watering along with daily harvesting. He attended three farmer's markets a week. Prepping for those—washing and packing up vegetables and herbs, loading them in Lance's pickup truck, and manning a booth in the hot sun for hours before packing it all up again, was exhausting. And there was still the bookkeeping to be done and planning and ordering for next season's crops, plus what hours he could steal to work on his hybrids. He'd grow squash, lettuce, kale, and brassicas until the snow hit. Over winter, he could limp along some of the sturdier plants in his greenhouse and in cold frames. And then in February, it would be time to start next year's seeds and the cycle would begin again.

Despite the long days, Tim had never been happier. He

wasn't exactly making a fortune, but he was selling well at the markets and bringing cash in. And he wasn't alone. Lily insisted on feeding him regularly, and Lance had hinted about moving into the cabin soon, renting out his little house in town. For the first time in possibly forever, Tim wasn't fearful of the future. He felt secure, that life was something great he was building rather than a road to nowhere.

So of course, that was when Marshall showed up.

Tim and Gus were winding down the Mad Creek farmer's market at three in the afternoon. Tim was rearranging the last of the peppers on their table, when he heard a snide voice.

"Those look like Lemonade Poppers."

Tim looked up into Marshall's irritated face and felt his stomach drop. "Oh. Hi, Marshall. Nice to see you too. They're not Lemonade Poppers, for your information. They're Golden Bells. Victory Seeds. They're much larger, and darker gold too."

Marshall looked at the gold sweet peppers with a put-upon frown, as though Tim were lying. The guy really didn't know his fucking vegetables, did he?

"Just because you're up here in the mountains doesn't mean you can get away with stealing from me," Marshall began.

"My lawyer says if you've got a business license, we can have it revoked for copyright infringement. We can make it illegal for you to sell produce anywhere in California! And you signed a non-disclosure when you worked for me. If you so much as breathe a word of what you did when you worked for Roots of Life—and I know you already told Linda Fitzgibbons—I can sue you for whatever pathetic dregs of cash you still have. So if I were you…"

Marshall ranted on, essentially telling Tim he wasn't allowed to grow anything, anywhere, anytime, til the end of his days. Tim tuned him out as he drew out his phone and calmly sent a text message. Then he stood and listened some more, nodding encouragement and asking the occasional stupid question to keep Marshall going. He folded his arms over his chest and suppressed a smile.

Because Marshall… Marshall had no idea what was about to hit him. *Wow, it sucks to be you right now.* It was so great! And suddenly Tim saw Marshall's problem for what it was. He'd lost control over Tim and over his hybrids, which was the one thing that had made Roots of Life a success. He'd probably thought he could manipulate Tim for years to come. And he was likely scared, too, that Tim would tell people the hybrids were

312

his, and about how he'd been treated, that he would tarnish the company's reputation.

Marshall was going on about the Roots' customer mailing list, which Tim didn't even have, when Janine, looking very proper in a charcoal suit and purple shirt, tapped him on the shoulder.

Marshall turned to glance at her, his hippy dreads bouncing, then did a double take.

"Oh. Excuse me, Miss, but if you're wanting to buy vegetables, you'd best find another table. This man has stolen from me. He doesn't have a right to sell any of this."

Janine raised one pricelessly cold eyebrow. "Defamation of character. Interesting." She handed him a white card. "Janine Donegal, attorney. Mr. Weston is my client. And you, sir, are way out of line."

Marshall took the card and read it carefully, as if that would prove it was all a joke. But apparently, the card looked legit, because he frowned. "I've already spoken to *my* lawyer about this, Ms. Donegal. If you have any point to make, you can make it to him."

"I quite agree," Janine said smoothly. "And in fact, if *you*

313

have any point to make, you can make it to *me*. From now on, I would ask you not to speak directly to my client, ever. Not by phone, not via email, and certainly not in person. It goes without saying that threatening him at his place of business will be taken for the criminal act it is."

Marshall shot Tim a dirty look, but he was slowly deflating as it became obvious he wasn't going to be able to run over Tim the way he used to.

"And, to avoid a lot of wasted time," Janine continued briskly. "I can tell you that Mr. Weston has shared all of his employment contracts with me. The language borders on illegal, and I have several issues with the validity of the execution, which I'll be taking up with your lawyer. But even assuming the contract *is* enforceable, you have absolutely no right to preclude my client from growing anything from publicly offered seed companies and selling the fruits of those plants. And that includes the seeds of his own hybrids that *you* are now selling to your customer base via mail order. He can legally grow those seeds, and sell the produce, til the cows come home. And, to be clear, as Tim develops new hybrids you have no stake in them, not since the day he formally terminated his employment with you, which was March 10th of this year."

314

"That's… that's not precisely—"

"Oh, it is *precisely*. I'm so glad you stopped by to let me witness in person your verbal threats. I'll be mailing a letter to your lawyer today outlining my client's rights and requesting a cease and desist of your continued harassment. And I'll send a copy to you at your place of business as well, of course."

Janine was so… puffed up, bristled, that Tim felt a little sorry for Marshall. He was glad he wasn't on Janine's bad side.

"We'll see about this," Marshall threatened lamely, but he was already backing away.

He backed right into Lance, who was standing, watching, feet braced, in full sheriff's uniform, completed with mirrored shades. Marshall spun around to see what he'd hit.

"Oh. Sorry, Officer."

"Sheriff. I'm the *sheriff*."

Marshall blinked at Lance's hard tone. "Oh. Sorry, Sheriff. Everything's fine. I was just—"

Lance grabbed fistfuls of Marshall's tie-dyed shirt in both hands and lifted him a few inches off the ground. "It's not fine. At all. I heard you just threaten *my boyfriend*." There was a deadly poison dripping off every word, and his lips drew back to reveal his strong white teeth.

Tim put a shocked hand over his mouth to hold in a laugh.

"Your...? I'm... No, I—"

"This is what's going to happen. I'm going to drive you to the town line. And then I'm going to send you over it. Head first. And if you ever step foot in *my* town again, or contact *my* boyfriend Tim again, I will find you and you will regret it. You're lucky I don't kick your ass right now for that bullshit you pulled on him when he worked for you."

"But... but...."

Lance turned and marched toward his cruiser, which was sitting, lights flashing, in the parking lot. He kept Marshall mid-air as if he weighed nothing. Marshall's hands flailed as he tried to explain. The crowd parted for them, the pack members watching with intent focus, ready to step in should Marshall do anything stupid. Or stupider anyway.

"Well. He's a tool," Janine said with a huff.

"That's Marshall," Tim said, still suppressing the giggles. God, he was a bad person, but he just fucking *loved* this. Maybe it wasn't revenge against his father, Tim realized in a moment of self-understanding. But it was close enough to feel pretty damn good.

"He won't be back," Tim said. "He's a total chickenshit."

"I'll make sure of it. If Lance leaves anything breathing, that is."

Lily ran up, her eyes wild. "I heard! Where is he? Where is that damn bastard?"

"Lance took care of it, Lily. Him and Janine. It's fine." Tim was a little alarmed by the look of eager rage on Lily's face.

"But I wanted to!" Lily sounded genuinely offended at being left out. She jumped up and down.

"Lance took him to the parking lot. Don't think they've left yet," Gus said helpfully.

Lily's eyes lit up, and she took off toward the parking lot like a bat out of hell. Or a border collie after a fox, maybe.

"Yup, I don't think Marshall will be bothering you again," Janine said drolly, watching Lily go.

Tim finally allowed himself to laugh out loud. He picked up a Golden Bells pepper and tossed it in the air, took a bite.

Mad Creek—crazy, wonderful, *pack*. He was home.

The End

About Eli Easton

ELI EASTON has been at various times and under different names a minister's daughter, a computer programmer, a game designer, the author of paranormal mysteries, a fanfiction writer, an organic farmer, and a profound sleeper. She is now happily embarking on yet another incarnation, this time as an m/m romance author.

As an avid reader of such, she is tickled pink when an author manages to combine literary merit, vast stores of humor, melting hotness, and eye-dabbing sweetness into one story. She promises to strive to achieve most of that most of the time. She currently lives on a farm in Pennsylvania with her husband, three bulldogs, three cows, and six chickens. All of them (except for the husband) are female, hence explaining the naked men that have taken up residence in her latest fiction writing.

Her website is http://www.elieaston.com.
You can e-mail her at eli@elieaston.com
Twitter is @EliEaston

"HOWL AT THE MOON" #2
Will be published November 2015
It will be Roman's story

24577746R00182

Made in the USA
San Bernardino, CA
29 September 2015